W9-AWE-043

Hoffmann

RENDERING

A CYBERSKUNKS POST

joel naftali

EGMONT EGMONT **EGMONT**
USA
NEW YORK

EGMONT

We bring stories to life

First published by Egmont USA, 2011
443 Park Avenue South, Suite 806
New York, NY 10016

1 3 5 7 9 8 6 4 2

www.egmontusa.com

Library of Congress Cataloging-in-Publication Data
Naftali, Joel.
The rendering / Joel Naftali.
p. cm.
Summary: Thirteen-year-old Doug relates in a series of blog posts the story
of how he saved the world but was falsely branded a terrorist and murderer,
forced to fight the evil Dr. Roach and his armored biodroid army with an
electronics-destroying superpower of his own.
ISBN 978-1-60684-118-1 (hardcover) — 978-1-60684-276-8 (eBook)
[1. Science fiction. 2. Adventure and adventurers—Fiction. 3. Blogs—Fiction.]
I. Title.
PZ7.N13354Re 2011
[Fic]—dc22
2010036640

Printed in the United States of America

CPSIA tracking label information:
Random House Production · 1745 Broadway · New York, NY 10019

THE RENDERING

IS ANYONE OUT THERE?

Well, I guess *you're* reading this.

Would you do me a favor and leave a comment saying how you found the blog? You probably searched for my name, except this Web site isn't even in the top three thousand search results for "Doug Solomon."

Unlike a hundred other blogs, all written by people pretending they're me. But I'm the genuine article:

- the kid with the $100,000 reward on his head, even though he's only got $40 to his name.
- the kid featured on *America's Most Dangerous*, even though he's not guilty.

Maybe that's why you're here. You think I killed my aunt. You think I'm a fugitive from justice, a homicidal maniac, or a domestic terrorist.

A thirteen-year-old driven crazy by video games.

Or maybe you're not sure. Maybe you're one of those conspiracy theorists who don't believe everything they see on TV.

Maybe you think I'm innocent. That I didn't bomb the Center, that I didn't kill anyone.

The only problem is, if you think *that*, you probably also think the explosion originated from an alien mother ship.

Yeah, the only people who believe I'm not a killer also believe in flying saucers.

Well, I'm not an alien and I'm not a psycho or a terrorist.

Sure, I'm living under a fake name now, in an undisclosed location, but I'm just an ordinary kid.

At least, I *was*.

A COMMENT ON COMMENTS

No comments yet. Maybe because nobody's reading this.

Or maybe you're scared.

Maybe you heard about someone who disappeared: a random guy online, a fellow gamer, an aunt. That's why I'm writing this: to tell you what's really going on. To explain what really happened to *my* aunt—and to the others who vanished.

Don't worry about commenting. Nobody can track you from this site.

If they could track *you*, they would've caught *me* in the past few months since my whole life blew up in my face. Good thing those pictures on *America's Most Dangerous* were taken when I was in the first grade. And they're the most recent photos, because all digital images of me were altered or destroyed. For my protection.

Anyway, I'll post as often as I can. That is, when I'm not running from monkeybeasts or wrestling with my homework.

THE REGULAR SPOT

I guess I'll begin at the regular spot—the beginning. Back when I was an ordinary kid, my days started like this:

1. Wake twenty minutes late and throw on some clothes. Preferably not the same ones as the day before. Well, preferably not *all* the same ones as the day before.
2. Wait at the bus stop, playing my GamePod. Sit in the middle of the bus. Not in front with nerds, not in back with bullies.
3. Math: Beat level twelve while playing under desk. GamePod confiscated.
4. English: Stare outside at the playing field.
5. Social studies: Revolutionary War again. Still boring after all these years.

6. P.E.: Run back and forth on the basketball court, trying to blend in. Shoot twice, score once.
7. Art: The kiln goes haywire and melts the sculptures. Pretty cool.
8. Science: Nothing goes haywire. Boring.
9. Play *Arsenal Five* after school while my best friend researches our social studies project.
10. Dinner and TV, more games, and bed. Oh, and homework. Maybe.

That was my life, in ten easy steps. Probably not all that different from yours.

At least, back then.

But now I'm posting from an anonymous server and routing my messages across the world a million times. And I left that school; I left that town; I left everything behind. I even have a new name now, one I can't tell you.

Because I don't want to look up from my desk in math class one day to see a biodroid swivel its plated head around the room scanning for me.

On the list of things I don't want, that rates pretty high.

WITH THE SOUL OF A GARBAGE DISPOSAL

Still no comments, so I can only guess what you want to know. Let's start with, what's a biodroid?

Think *vicious* and *armored*: a cross between a pit bull and a tank. Some are the size of your average ninth grader, others the size of your average dump truck.

Oh, and they have missile launchers.

And flamethrowers.

And bad attitudes.

And they've hacked into every security camera, database, and computer system in the country.

Before all this started, my biggest problems were passing tests and beating video games, not an army of killer cyborgs hunting me down. But now? I might look like an ordinary kid, but according to VIRUS, I'm Public Enemy Number One.

That's the bad news.

The good news is I've got friends.

SUCH A NICE TOWN

Wait, I meant to tell you about my normal life first.

I lived in a small town not too far from a small city in—you guessed it—a small state. A nice little town exactly like every other nice little town.

With one difference.

Well, you found this blog, so you already know parts of my story. You know where I'm from, and you know about the smoldering crater I left behind.

But you don't know this: tucked away in the outskirts of my nice little town, behind security fences and minefields, you would've found the Biodigital Research Center.

Not the "Center for Medical Innovation," despite what the signs said. *Not* an organization that developed cutting-edge medical technology. *Not* a building guarded by layers of security to keep the experimental germs inside.

No, you would've found the Biodigital Research Center, funded by a government program so secret that even the CIA didn't know about it.

Because it should've been called the Biodigital *Top Secret Weapons Development* Research Center.

Get the idea?

Yeah, I thought you might.

My aunt Margaret used to work there. She was an expert in tachyon mapping, subatomic interfaces, stuff like that. I'll skip the technical details, but—

You do not understand the technical details, Douglas.

Thanks for the vote of confidence. That was my aunt—or what's left of her—hacking my Net connection again.

Only to monitor the security of your link and ensure your safety. You know the searchbots never stop hunting for you.

I'll explain later how Aunt Margaret hacks the Net, if she can manage to keep from interrupting.

I will try to restrain myself.

Thanks.

Back when life was normal, Aunt Margaret worked at the Center, doing high-tech top secret stuff. Of course, she never told me exactly what she did other than "medical research"—that's why it's called top *secret*—but I've learned a lot since then.

I used to hang at her office sometimes, just in the public areas, not the archives or the tech-development labs. And if you're expecting to hear that I followed in her footsteps, that I'm some boy genius, let me disappoint you right now: I'm barely passing science.

I'm not an athlete; I'm not a gifted student; I'm not a singer or an artist or a poet.

I'm a regular kid. Just like you.

A MELTDOWN IN ART CLASS

Well, except for one little quirk.

Remember that kiln that went haywire and ruined all the sculptures in art class? I guess I wasn't *completely* ordinary, even back then. Things like that sometimes . . . happened around me.

The first time I remember, I was six years old. My remote-control car smashed itself into pieces against the fridge, ignoring the controls completely. Then cell phones stopped working and cameras malfunctioned. Not always, but often enough that I learned not to stick around for group photographs. When a camcorder bursts into flames every few years, you start to notice.

Other than *that*, though? Call me Mr. Ordinary.

FREE FIRE

You want to know *why* I'd hang around an office building instead of watching TV at home? I mean, considering I'm not exactly the Einstein Kid, eager for some alone time in a science lab. And considering they didn't let me into the top secret areas, just the parts that looked like any other boring big business.

Video games.

An entire wall of them, a long line stretching down the length of the employee lounge in the Center. All flashing, beeping, whirring, and absolutely free:

ARSENAL FIVE
SMASH AND GRAB III
XTREME RACER 500
ĦÅƘƤ

The employee lounge smelled of microwave popcorn, and sometimes my aunt's coworkers chatted at me, but still: free video games.

Heaven.

So that's why I was there that day.

And, um, I don't want to get all Movie of the Week, but sometimes I don't like being alone. The thing is, my parents died in a car crash when I was a little kid, so I lived with Auntie M, just the two of us. I used to call her that, to make her laugh. *Auntie M.* And because, you know, there's no place like home.

I guess I'm supposed to be depressed about my parents, but I don't even remember them. So Auntie M is my whole family.

Well, she *was.* Whatever.

At least I still have Jamie.

THE GIRL NEXT DOOR

Looking back, I realize that living with my aunt was great. And that was how I met Jamie, because she lived next door. I don't want to give her a big head or anything, but . . . you know how I keep saying I'm a regular guy?

Jamie is different. Irregular.

Well, maybe she's not that bad, but she was a little too rich and way too smart to fit in at our school. She wore designer clothes while the other girls wore chain store stuff. She rode a Diamond Royce bike instead of a Huffy. And I'm not sure if she's officially a genius, but she took calculus in the sixth grade.

Plus she's one of those kids who, for some reason, deal with adults better than they do with other kids.

For example, my aunt's the one who introduced us.

DON'T MESS WITH THE BARBIE

When I was in elementary school, I came back from dirt biking one day and shoved through the front door. "I'm home!"

"In here," Auntie M called from her study.

I poured a bowl of cereal in the kitchen and found them in the study: my aunt and this girl wearing a floofy pink dress and pink tights. Jamie denies this, but I swear there were at least three bows in her hair. All pink.

"This is Jamie from next door," my aunt said. "She's helping with my filing."

"Why?" I asked, crunching my cereal.

"Because you didn't want to."

"No, I mean, what's in it for her?"

"When I grow up," the girl told me, "I'm gonna be a scientist. I'm gonna be just like your aunt."

I ate another spoonful. "I don't think so."

"Why not?"

"Because my aunt doesn't look like an explosion in a Barbie factory."

So Jamie hurled a book at my head. Not much aim, but plenty of power.

RISE OF THE ROOT CANAL

My aunt had the window repaired, and Jamie outgrew her pink phase. Mostly. And over the next year, we became best friends. I'm still not exactly sure how; it doesn't matter anymore.

I just knew that clearing a level on *Arsenal Five* was more fun when Jamie was at her laptop, memorizing the periodic table or whatever she did before VIRUS destroyed our lives. Kicking back and watching TV was better with her, too.

Plus, in her post-pink phase, Jamie was willing to get her hands dirty. For example, she was up for going to these empty lots near our street to race dirt bikes and light firecrackers and rebuild an old laser printer.

Well, that last one was Jamie's idea. I'd wanted to smash the printer with hammers.

Anyway, I went poking around one day and found the basement of a house that used to be there. A dark, mildewed, slimy cave. I was ten years old at the time and thought it was the best thing ever.

My aunt found out and didn't care. Told you she was cool. In fact, she gave the place a nickname: the root canal. Because it was like a root cellar, but painful as a toothache. Don't get me started on my aunt's sense of humor.

For two weeks that summer, Jamie and I worked on the basement: shoveling, laying down a plywood floor, dragging an old couch into the hole.

Jamie wanted to install wireless.

Then a rainstorm hit, and the root canal turned into a mud pit.

The thing is, Jamie didn't exactly love hanging around a nasty abandoned basement, but she spent two weeks remodeling the root canal because she knew I wanted to. And I don't care about science, but if she needs help measuring the effect of magnetism on mitochondrial output, I'm game.

And I don't even know what *mitochondrial* means.

I guess that's enough background. The point is, my life was pretty great back then: good friends, free video games, and no worries.

And I loved my aunt. I never would've done anything to hurt her.

AN ORDINARY DAY

So where should I start? That morning, I guess, the morning everything changed.

The alarm went off, as usual. And ten minutes later, my aunt opened my bedroom door: "Time for school."

"Mmph."

She prodded my covers with a hockey stick. "You're going to miss the bus."

I rubbed my eyes. "It's Saturday."

"In what universe?"

I shook away the last bits of my dream. Something about it being Saturday, and me getting the high score on *Xtreme Racer 500*. "Oh."

"Welcome to Wednesday," she said. "Get dressed."

Downstairs, I reached for the cereal and saw a pizza box on the kitchen table. Three slices left from the night before—but Auntie M didn't usually think pizza was an appropriate breakfast food.

"What's this for?" I asked.

"Breakfast."

"What's the catch?"

She sighed. "I may need to work late for the next few weeks."

"Oh." I grabbed a slice. "You're feeling guilty. Is this a bribe?" I looked at the pizza. "Maybe I should hold out for a Zii game console."

"I could get a babysitter instead," she mused.

"No, pizza's great! We're good."

"You drive a hard bargain," she said.

Which was typical. Auntie M had never wanted kids, but she managed surrogate motherhood the same way she did everything else: like a science experiment.

Douglas!

Kidding, kidding! Wire yourself a funny bone.

No, my aunt and I liked living together. I'm not saying we never fought—we did, but not often. We just sort of . . . got along.

Anyway, after the pizza, I reached the bus stop three minutes early, then took a seat in the middle and watched Jamie's house slip past. Her parents always dropped her at school an hour before first bell, for advanced tutoring.

The day was warm, so at lunchtime Jamie and I and some other kids went outside and ate at the stone fence.

I hardly remember what we talked about. Nothing much, I guess.

Your biology project.

Oh, right! Jamie wanted to stay after school to finish the research. "The project's due next week," she said.

"That's plenty of time," I told her.

"What's the project?" another kid asked.

"Entomology," Jamie said. "Insects. We haven't even chosen which one yet."

THE DRAGONFLY

I grinned. "Sure we have. Gimme."

She handed me her laptop, and I tapped a few keys, then showed her the screen. She read aloud:

> The dragonfly spends most of its life in the
> nymph form, beneath the water's surface.
> Nymphs use extendable jaws to hunt. They
> breathe through gills and rapidly propel

themselves by expelling water through the . . .
(Jamie glanced at me, then changed the next
word) backside.

"Butt propulsion," I said.

Everyone started laughing.

"Plus," I continued, "they're the world's fastest insect.
Clocked at sixty-two miles an hour."

Jamie rolled her eyes. "Well, that's a rigorous scientific
reason to study them. How about we do honeybees?"

"No, listen to this." I scrolled down. "Dragonflies use
an optical illusion called motion camouflage to stalk other
insects. They look like stationary objects while attacking
prey."

I knew she couldn't resist that: Jamie liked strange interactions of complex systems.

Me? I liked butt propulsion.

AN ORDINARY DAY, CONTINUED

Then we went inside for more classes; then we went home.
You know—an ordinary day, like most of my days before I
started living under a fake identity. Before I started appearing
in headlines:

VIDEO GAMES DROVE BOY TO MURDER
THE AFTERMATH: FROM HYPERACTIVE TO HOMICIDAL
BOY HOPED TO SLAY 666 NEIGHBORS

Then there were the grainy screenshots on TV, of a blur-faced kid wearing my favorite T-shirt and sneaking a bomb into the Center. It's amazing how VIRUS can manipulate video. I almost believed them myself.

After dinner, I tagged along with Auntie M to the Center. She drove through town, then the two miles of no-man's-land, before hitting the outermost security fence.

She passed the first two guard shacks by flashing her ID.

"If you need to spend the night," I said, "I can take the shuttle bus home."

She shook her head. "Shouldn't take more than a few hours, unless the wetware interface is acting up."

We waited at the automated guard shack while a bio-resonant scanner checked that we were actually Margaret and Doug Solomon.

"Jamie said something about a biology project?" she said when the crash gates opened. "On insects?"

"Dragonflies. I'll do some research tonight." The Center had priority access to every database in the world—even from the unclassified areas they let me into—which really made school projects easier.

"Don't expect Jamie to write the paper for you."

"I *said* I'll do the research."

"E-mailing her search results isn't enough." Auntie M pulled into her parking space. "Don't make her do all the work."

"Yeah, because I'm too stupid to help write the paper."

"Doug, I never said—"

"You don't think I'm stupid." I shoved open my door. "You think I'm lazy."

"You *are* lazy!"

I slammed the door and stormed through the visitors' entrance. A stupid fight, the kind that doesn't mean anything, just blowing off steam.

Then why did I even mention it?

Because that was our last real conversation.

THE CENTER CANNOT HOLD

Here's a pop quiz. After slamming from the car, did I:

A) head immediately to the only unclassified library
   in the Center to start researching dragonflies?

B) find an empty office and sit in the corner
   weeping, because nobody understood me?

C) go directly to the employee lounge, flick the

Start button on *Arsenal Five*, and blast away
with the carapace rifle?

Yeah, too easy.

After I incinerated a few levels on *Arsenal Five*, I played two arcs of *HARP*. That stands for *High-Altitude Recon Protocol*, if you didn't already know, and the game's based on real NASA research of the upper atmosphere using instruments shot from a cannon.

Seriously. That's what they do at NASA.

The game starts at home base, where you're briefed and you choose your gear. Then they launch you into suborbit and you arc through the atmosphere, incinerating the baddies and racing against the clock until—

Pardon me, Douglas, but is this information essential?

Well, I guess it's not *essential*.

Is it relevant in any way whatsoever?

Um, not really. I mean, unless you're playing *HARP*. If anyone's playing *HARP*, I know some killer shortcuts. E-mail me.

Perhaps you might focus on matters more directly related to the upcoming events?

Sure. Good point. Where was I?

Oh, right. After *HARP*, I started my current favorite game: *Street Gang*.

I don't know if you've played *Street Gang*. First you choose which gang you want to be (I chose the Hog Stompers, a biker gang) and which gang you want to fight (in this case, the Fists of Kung Fu, these ninja warriors).

Most people like the Fists better than the Hogs, because the ninjas are, well, *ninjas*. They've got a killer stealth attack, and their throwing stars are awesome.

But the Hogs can soak an endless amount of damage, and the limited-range attack with the motorcycle chains is devastating, if you know how to use it.

Which I do.

The best way is by—

Again, Douglas. Relevance?

Hey! You *know Street Gang* is relevant. I'm living with a ninja-powered biker chick as I type this.

Indeed. But the mechanics of specific attacks?

Fine, fine. Just trying to help.

Anyway, that's the employee lounge: basically a video arcade with a snack bar attached. Plus an exercise room and a bunch of couches and a digital banner right below the ceiling:

HAPPY 37TH BIRTHDAY ELISE N!!! . . .
DON'T FORGET—SOFTBALL PRACTICE IS
NOW ON WEDNESDAY . . . CONGRATS TO

```
WALTER P, EMPLOYEE OF THE MONTH! . . .
HAPPY 37TH BIRTHDAY ELISE N!!! . . .
DON'T FORGET—SOFTBALL PRACTICE IS
NOW ON WEDNESDAY . . . CONGRATS TO
WALTER P, EMPLOYEE OF THE MONTH! . . .
```

As for the Center itself, picture an *enormous* warehouse with an office building attached, surrounded by two miles of no-man's-land, four fences, and a minefield.

And for that extra layer of security, a dozen biodigital tanks.

What are those? Picture an Abrams tank with steel-plate armor and a rotating turret—except run by an artificial intelligence as vicious as a junkyard dog.

A BIODIGITAL INTERLUDE

I'm not gonna pretend I understand exactly what *biodigital* means, or Auntie M will interrupt again. But the basic idea is transforming biological stuff—brain stems, nervous systems, animal instinct—into digital code.

And there are only three good reasons why you're reading this blog.

1. You want to know why I killed my aunt. You

want to look inside the mind of a killer, to discover what turned a regular kid into a terrorist.

2. You figure I didn't kill my aunt and want to know what happened to her. What happened to my entire town? And are *you* gonna disappear next?

3. You heard about the skunks. Maybe you saw one of the video captures and didn't dismiss the whole thing as a hoax.

Well, biodigital technology is the key to the skunks. So if you're here for reason number three, this is how it works:

First you translate biological systems into digital code. Then you combine that code with cutting-edge hardware (and wetware and fluxware). And congratulations, you've stumbled through a hidden door into the future of technology!

Maybe an example will help.

Say you want to create a world-class fugitive tracker. You digitize a bloodhound's sense of smell, to get a scent-hunting ability that's generations beyond anything you could invent. Then you build a handheld "sniffer" that uses that bloodhound-based software, and *ta-da!*

A fully networked, portable man hunter that doesn't stop to pee on trees. Plus you throw in night vision, maybe sonar from a bat, and whatever else strikes your fancy.

That's the basic idea, the beta version of biodigital tech. The more advanced applications are endless, and dangerous. And like nothing the world's ever seen.

You know those videos of the skunks that appear on YouTube for a few minutes before someone crashes the whole site? They're not hoaxes. They're not jokes.

They're snapshots from a secret war.

BACK TO THE CENTER

Inside—at least in the public areas, the unclassified zones where the secretaries worked and the nephews visited—the Center looked like a regular office building, with water-coolers and workstations and cubicles. My aunt was the head of research, so her office, on the second floor, had windows and a Persian rug and a comfy couch.

Wandering around, you wouldn't stumble on anything interesting. Well, except for the armored doors and **NO ENTRY** signs. And the guards with assault rifles.

Other than *that*, though, just your ordinary office building.

To tell the truth, I'd never wanted to get behind those locked doors. I figured you could search for a month and not find anything cooler than a Bunsen burner.

Well, I learned later that night how wrong I'd been. Because behind those doors, down wide bright hallways, you'd walk right into:

- the BattleArmor development lab,
- virtual reality combat simulators, and
- the animal research section.

In the BattleArmor lab, they'd built a prototype suit that would turn an ordinary soldier into a tank. Think RoboCop crossed with Iron Man. There was just one problem: nobody could wear the armor.

They needed a soldier genetically designed for the suit, and that was generations beyond their abilities. Or so they thought.

As for the virtual reality combat simulators: if I'd known that *those* were behind the locked doors, I'd have broken in somehow. Because they were the ultimate video games, offering complete immersion in millions of combat scenarios, to train elite Special Forces soldiers.

At least, in theory. In practice, they hadn't deployed the sims, because they were *too* realistic. Users might actually die of simulated wounds. That's like if you really broke your leg every time you fell off a roof in *Smash and Grab III*.

And finally, the animal research section. They had rabbits and parakeets and snakes and monkeys and beetles and on and on.

of the continental United States has highly, extremely, or absolutely limited surveillance-reconstruction potential.

Well, I said *almost*. Sheesh.

So that's the setup. And this is how everything came crashing down.

THE BAD DOCTOR

Other than me, my aunt, and a few guards, the Center was empty. At least, that's what the sensors recorded . . . but they missed the man in the animal research section.

Dr. Ronald J. Roach: a bony, thin-lipped creep with cold eyes and a colder heart. And an IQ too high to measure.

There's no record of how he entered the building. He used to work at the Center, until he was fired for conducting unauthorized experiments. Security cameras—which cover every inch of the place—went mysteriously dark and Auntie M presumes he smuggled himself inside during that period, hidden in one of the biodigital tanks he designed.

I presume nothing. I simply state that the probability of his having done so approaches 91.62 percent.

Anyway—

I would be pleased to see scores exceeding 90 percent on the papers you bring home from school, Douglas.

Okay, okay, I'll finish my homework as soon as I'm done with this.

You mean start your homework.

Do you want me conjugating Latin verbs or warning people that the country—the *world*—is in danger?

Preferably both.

Anyway, my aunt thinks Roach used a secret override code to hitch a ride inside one of the tanks. Then he let himself into the animal research section and walked down the rows of cages, rattling his pen along the bars. The animals knew him, and they feared him. They cowered and hissed as he passed.

"Seventeen minutes," he said, glancing at his watch. Yeah, he's such a mad scientist he actually talks to himself. "Then the second stage begins."

He rattled a few more bars, and a little white rabbit bounded away and trembled in the corner.

Roach glared at the bunny. "I should take your foot for good luck." He didn't do anything to the rabbit, though. Instead, he checked the device in his hand and said, "And now for the final procedure." His icy gaze probed the room. "Should I use the hamsters? The monkeys?" He crept down a few rows, then stopped. "Ah! The skunks."

He tapped on a keypad attached to the cage containing three skunks. There was a label on their cage:

L A R K S P U R	C O S M O	P O P P Y

Some clown had named the skunks after flowers.

Hilarious.

A robot arm scooped the skunks from their cage and deposited them in a clear tube. They scrabbled against the sides but couldn't grab anything, and in a moment, the tube retracted into the center of the Quantum Bio-Map Generator.

Roach dialed the power to critical levels, and a warning light flashed. He didn't care; he wasn't running a real test. He'd already taken control of the automated security and now needed to overload the communications systems so nobody could call for help.

Then he entered a password and a computer voice said, "Test authorized. Scanning bio-forms . . . Digitizing . . . Imaging . . . Please wait. . . ."

GRAYBAR AND GUNFIRE

"Scanning . . . Digitizing . . . Rendering . . . Rendering . . ."

Inside the machine, the skunks were being transformed

into patterns of subatomic particles and encoded as digital information.

Sure, that's clear.

Basically, the machine downloaded three skunk brains into computer files. Every instinct and memory was written onto software. Meanwhile, their furry little skunk bodies went limp, into a deep unnatural sleep, with only the machine keeping them alive.

Nothing could live for long after having its brain digitized. Well, not *yet*.

But what was happening *inside* the machine wasn't very important right then. Because *outside* the machine, a warning chime sounded on Aunt Margaret's computer.

"'Test authorized'?" Auntie M murmured to herself. She knew that nobody was authorized to run tests, not right then. "'System overload'?"

A map of the Center appeared on her screen, with the animal research section flashing. She frowned, stood from her workstation, and headed into the hallway.

She trotted around a corner, through a sliding security door, and past one of the guard stations. Maybe if she hadn't been distracted by wondering who'd authorized the test, she would've noticed that the guard stations were empty.

The guard stations were *never* empty.

But she didn't notice. She hurried into the animal research

section, where she heard the Quantum Bio-Map Generator humming. She crossed toward the machine, then saw that she wasn't alone.

"Roach!" she said. "What are you doing here?"

He smiled coldly. "Tidying up some loose ends."

"You were banned from the Center. Get out."

"After all the trouble I took to get *in*?"

"You're lucky they only banned you," she said. "They should've tossed you in jail—you know that scanning an entire organism into the databanks kills the subject. Your reckless experiments—"

"Those 'reckless experiments' are the future," he said. "Who are *they* to fire *me*, the greatest mind in ten generations? I'll show them. I'll show you all. Did they think I'd crawl into a hole to lick my wounds? No, I sold my technology to the highest bidder. I bought equipment on the black market and I continued my work. My scanning booths are operational. You'll see—all you meatpeople, you'll see what true genius is!"

"Stop with the crazy talk," Auntie M said, crossing to the security button on the wall. "You're breaking the law just being inside the perimeter."

"I write my own laws."

She pressed the button, but nothing happened. No alarm, no alert. She turned slowly back to Roach, her eyes worried.

"Ah," he said with another cold smile. "You begin to understand."

"You disabled the security."

"You can't imagine I'm here on a whim." He glanced at his watch. "No, this is planned to the millisecond."

"What do you want, Roach?"

"First the Protocol," he said. "Then the HostLink. How does that sound?"

Auntie M snorted. "Over my dead body."

"Now that," Roach said, taking a gun from his pocket, "is a deal."

And he pulled the trigger.

THE VOCAB

Okay, so what are the HostLink and the Protocol?

The Center's top technicians had been working on the HostLink for years, trying to build a machine that could digitize minds from a distance. They planned to use it as a research tool so scientists in the United States could work with teams in Japan and Norway.

They'd just gotten a prototype working—which, I later realized, was why Roach finally attacked. He knew how to make the HostLink hijack any device connected to the Net, to scan in minds through Web-enabled cell phones and desktop PCs. Thousands of minds at a time. Maybe millions.

And you've probably never heard of the Protocol, either— the Biogenic Protocol, the most advanced software produced by the Center. My aunt and Roach had slaved over that code for years, before Roach went insane.

Or *more* insane. He was never what you'd call a poster boy for mental health.

So what *is* the Protocol? Some kind of programming wizardry that switches seamlessly between digital and biological systems.

In other words, I'm not sure. But my aunt said the Protocol was the closest thing to a magic wand you'd find in the digital world. Kind of a universal translator, able to convert brain waves, for example, into software.

That is hardly what I said, Douglas.

Well, close enough. If anyone wants more info <coughgeekcough>, click the link that says *Protocol*.

All that really matters is this: in the right hands, the HostLink and Protocol are stunning technological advances. But in the wrong hands, they're deadly weapons that bring biodigital monsters to life and transform real people into digital code. And when people are reduced to code, they don't just die: their minds are stolen, transformed into processors more powerful than the most cutting-edge computer, and exploited by the person who scanned them.

Only two things limited the HostLink and Protocol's power: the user's skills and imagination. Which kinda sucked, because Roach coded better than anyone alive, and he imagined bloodthirsty hordes of biodroid soldiers.

READY, FIRE, AIM

Back to Roach, pulling the trigger.

Now, nobody doubts that Roach is a stone genius. As far as pure brainpower, the guy's basically unrivaled.

But you know what? He's still a crappy shot.

He fired at my aunt and hit the wall behind her. Then he fired again and hit the ceiling. No kidding. He took a breath and steadied the gun, and my aunt ducked behind an aquarium, and the next shot missed her and shattered the fish tank.

Water sloshed everywhere and dozens of guppies splashed to the floor.

Auntie M raced for the exit.

Roach fired three more shots as he ran toward her. He missed and missed and missed and lost his balance on the wet floor. He fell onto his butt and slid across the tile, through all the guppies flipping and flopping in the shallow puddles.

By the time he stood up again, Auntie M was long gone.

Doc Roach pressed a button on his communicator and said, "Commander Hund?"

AN UNFORTUNATE INTRODUCTION

At that point, I'd never even heard the name Hund, much less seen the man. Still, here's a little preview:

Hund probably isn't seven feet tall, but I bet he's close. He has dark hair and a scar across his face and usually about a hundred pounds of killing machines strapped to his body—a dozen weapons, each one deadlier than the next.

But that's not the worst part. The worst part is his eyes.

One glows yellow under some kind of an implanted lens. And the other stares at you like Randy Pinhurst (this freaky kid I knew in fifth grade) used to look at flies before he ripped off their wings.

Hund is the commander of Roach's mercenary army—and a recurring character in my nightmares.

EVERYTHING'S A BLUR

Roach murmured into his communicator: "Commander Hund?"

"We've neutralized the guards," Hund reported. "The building is ours."

"Not quite. Dr. Solomon is on the loose. I'm pushing the timetable forward."

"The explosives will be armed in five minutes," Hund said.

"Then I'm setting detonation for ten."

Roach tapped a few times on his communicator, and a digital display started running down in a blur.

10:00

9:59

9:58

9:57

9:56

You know how in movies the good guy always stops the timer when it's at 00:02 or something? I hate that. I always root for the bomb, and the bigger the explosion, the better.

Not this time.

This time, I wanted the timer to stop at 9:56.

Still, here's a little spoiler. Plenty of stuff happened in the next ten minutes: armed mercenaries, technological miracles, and digital murder. But one thing that didn't happen? A hero swinging into action and stopping that clock.

So pretty soon, that timer showed

00:09

00:08

00:07

00:06

00:05

00:04

00:03

00:02

00:01

Then the detonator fired.

BACK UP

When Roach had started scanning the skunks, I'd been sitting in Auntie M's office. Not her lab, of course; that was off-limits. But she'd given me a pass to visit the low-clearance offices, after I'd tagged along on an official tour the year before. I think she'd wanted to get me interested in science class.

Anyway, I'd finished playing *Street Gang*, and I was *bored*.

I'd surfed the Web for a while, but that had gotten stale fast, so I'd called Jamie.

"Hey," I said when she picked up.

"Don't tell me," she said. "You finished playing video games and now you're bored."

"That is completely unfair."

"So what's up?"

"I finished playing video games and now I'm bored."

Jamie laughed. "Then start the biology project. Unless you want to get a C-plus again."

"You sound like Auntie M."

"Yeah, and I'll be a world-famous cybernaut when you're just a loser video gamer."

We bickered for a while, like we usually did; then I decided to do what she said, like I usually did. I logged in to the Center's library on my aunt's computer. "I'll search the databases for dragonfly stuff," I told her, "and e-mail you what I find."

"Focus on that stealth flight ability," she said. "And their eyes. They have thirty thousand lenses in each eye."

"Is that a lot? How many do we have in each eye?"

"One."

"Oh." I snorted. "Insects."

"You ought to love this project," Jamie said. *"Bug."*

Yeah, the other kids sometimes called me Bug, because it rhymes with Doug, obviously, and because of what I said before. Things happen around me. Electronic stuff breaks down. Computers crash and DVDs freeze up. Kilns go haywire in art class and melt all the sculptures.

Have you ever walked down a sidewalk and the streetlights flickered when you passed? Happens to me all the time. And forget about using a microwave. I mean, usually they're fine—but every six months, one bursts into flames while nuking a pizza bagel.

That's why I like my pizzas delivered.

Amazingly, nothing had ever gone haywire at the Center.

Until that night.

"Let's see . . . eyes and flight," I said, tapping a few words into the search field. "Gimme a minute, I'll send you the results."

"Sure, and I'll end up doing all the work."

"You *like* work," I said.

"Doug . . . ," she said warningly. "Not this time."

"Fine. We'll work on it in school tomorrow."

She said okay, and I found a bunch of information about dragonflies. More than a bunch, actually: six gigabytes, including partial DNA mapping and six hours of video.

I liked the common nicknames best:

devil's needle	*vagrant emperor*	*scarce chaser*
waterfall redspot	*sigma darner*	*azure hawker*
golden spiketail	*wandering glider*	*dark mossback*

"Ready for the file?" I asked, and clicked Send.

"I've got *CircuitBoard* open," Jamie said. *CircuitBoard* is a girl game—no fists, no knives, no guns, no blood, no violence. You just try to connect these circuits before the time runs out. Thrilling. "Wait a second."

"Um," I said.

"Let me finish, or you'll mess with my Net connection."

"I already hit Send," I said. "Here it comes."

"Bug! I was at my high score."

And right then, the timer hit 00:00, and—

THE DETONATOR FIRED

The floor c o l l a p s e d

beneath

me

and

I

f

e

l

l

.

.

.

Back to Aunt Margaret. Before the detonator fired, she escaped Roach, raced to processing lab three, and locked herself inside.

She tried calling the cops, but all Center communications were frozen by that power-draining test on the skunks. She knew she didn't have much time, so she launched her personal encryption and burrowed into the system, desperate to stop Roach.

Desperate to keep him from getting the Protocol and the HostLink.

Two minutes later, a pounding sounded in the hallway. Then silence for a few seconds, until the door burst inward and Roach's mercenaries poured inside. Auntie M didn't even look up from her computer. She just tapped a few more keys and hit Enter.

The mercs pointed these futuristic-looking rifles at her— only the best for Roach's army. Although I didn't know it then, he'd spent the past few years working for shadowy corporations and Third World tyrants, multiplying his fortune and perfecting his own technologies. And designing weapons that violated every treaty and moral scruple.

But the mercs didn't fire; they grabbed Auntie M instead.

"Do you have any idea who you're working for?" she asked them.

"The guy who signs our checks," one said.

"Roach isn't just a guy, he's a madman."

The merc shoved her. "Shut up."

"And if he gets away with this . . ." She shook her head. "He's a madman with access to weapons the Pentagon's never even seen."

"Yeah?" the mercenary said. "Then I'm gonna ask for a raise."

Before she could reply, Roach stepped inside, murmuring into his communicator: "What do you mean you can't find the Protocol?"

"It's not here," Hund's voice said through the speaker.

"We need that Memory Cube, Commander. It's the key to everything."

Don't worry if you've never heard of a Memory Cube; they're not on the market yet and probably won't be for another twenty years. I've seen a few around the Center, though. They're about the size of a deck of cards and they store data like a hard drive or a USB stick. Except Memory Cubes are so advanced they make your laptop look like a number two pencil.

"Then tell me where to find it," Hund said.

"One moment." Roach clicked off his communicator and eyed my aunt. "You didn't get far."

"You're being videotaped, Roach," my aunt said. "You're

not going to get away with this." She was calm and unafraid. Amazing.

"I already have," Roach said. "I was right all along: my theory about uploading the human brain is correct. And soon, with my scanning booths and the HostLink, we'll be digitizing entire organisms. Mind and body both."

"Your experiments almost killed the test subjects—"

"Everything can be scanned in, Margaret," he interrupted, eyes shining. "Not just a few stray impulses. *Everything*."

"Even if that's true, it's not worth the risk."

"That's always been your problem." Roach sneered. "Lack of vision. I can digitize towns, states, entire countries. With the right tech, I'll scan in the world. Think of it!"

"I'll tell you what I think," Aunt Margaret said. "I think you're insane."

"A perfect world! No human error. Everything reduced to code, eternal and pure. Imagine a world without hunger or pain or death. Without ugly messes and stupid mistakes. No muss, no fuss, no disgusting fleshy bodies."

She looked at him and—I swear this is true—said, "If you want to get rid of disgusting fleshy bodies, go to the gym more often."

He glared at her. "And no disobedience. Everyone will follow the program. Everyone will have a function and will perform that function perfectly."

"Or what?" she asked.

"Or the programmer will modify the faulty code."

"You're gonna digitize people against their will," she said, realization dawning on her face. "Scan them into your machine, even if it kills them."

"They won't die. They'll be reborn in new forms, immortal and perfect. They'll expand my digital realm, making me stronger—so I can digitize more, and get stronger still. Until there is nothing left of this foul world but acres of supercomputers humming in my underground vaults. And on those computers, we'll live forever—in perfect order."

"And you'll delete the mind of anyone who objects?"

"Of course not. I'll merely debug them."

"You *are* insane," my aunt said.

"Madness and genius . . ." Roach grabbed a pair of handheld scanners, like those shock paddles you see on TV shows when doctors jolt someone back to life. "They're two sides of the same equation."

Then he pressed the paddles to my aunt's temples.

FALLING DOWN

You know what's worse than suddenly falling through the air? Suddenly *stopping*.

I hit the ground hard and groaned for a few seconds. Then I felt something digging into my face and realized I was clinging to Auntie M's computer—which was still, somehow, sending data to Jamie's laptop.

Directly under my aunt's office was the Holographic Hub, the main CPU of the Center. I'd peeked inside on that tour I mentioned, through the observation window, and you know what I saw?

Nothing.

An empty white room. But inside that room, every molecule, every electron and atom was imprinted with information, like a track on a CD. It looks empty, but it's coursing with energy, with data.

And I fell right into the middle of it.

I didn't know that the explosion—the *first* explosion, I mean, a thousand times weaker than the final blast—was a mercenary attack. I didn't know they'd targeted the blast to neutralize the backup security while sparing the rest of the building so they could steal the technology. I didn't know anything.

To be honest, I thought the explosion was probably *my* fault. Not that I really cared, because I suddenly remembered the sign on the hub's door: **HIGHLY VOLATILE—APPROACH WITH EXTREME CAUTION**.

I needed to get out of there.

Yet I couldn't even stand. My strength was gone, and I felt myself getting weaker every second. Being inside the hub sapped my strength, made my brain buzz and my vision blur.

I forced myself to roll over and crawled toward the door.

Locked.

I looked for something to smash the observation window with. Everything from Auntie M's office had fallen through the floor with me. I saw her chair ten feet away. A scattering of books from her shelves. A few drawers from her desk, with the contents spilled everywhere.

I dragged myself back to her computer, figuring I could use it to break the window. It took all my strength to cross those ten feet; then I was too weak to lift the monitor. Instead, I keeled over. I lay there, staring at the white floor and the white walls and a scattering of junk from Auntie M's drawers:

1. Paper clips and sticky notes and pens.
2. A bottle of vitamins.
3. An old smartphone, the screen now broken.
4. A framed picture of me as a baby with my parents.
5. A Memory Cube with an orange label.

I blinked a few times, first watching a strange foggy glow around the Memory Cube, then peering at the picture. They say I look like my father. He was tall and lanky with messy dark hair—and always smiling or laughing in every picture I'd ever seen.

I smiled back at him.

Then I collapsed.

MY CUBIST PERIOD

Roach pressed the paddles to my aunt's temples and pulled the triggers.

The machine hummed, and my aunt screamed. Then she fell to the floor, where she lay unmoving. He'd erased her brain, transferred every synapse through the paddles into the Center's data banks. But he hadn't formatted the mainframe to accept her data, so her mind would soon fade into the darkness of the hard drives. And a few minutes later, her body would shut down completely.

Roach stepped over her like she was yesterday's laundry. "Now, Hund," he said into his communicator, "explain the problem. You're having trouble with security?"

"No. We breached the vault easily enough."

"But didn't find the cube?"

"We found the cube," Hund said.

"Then what's the problem?"

"It's blank."

"*What?* Impossible. You have the wrong cube."

"I have the cube that the Protocol was saved onto." Hund's voice crackled over the communicator. "Exactly as described. Except it's blank."

"I need that Protocol." Roach stepped up to a keyboard and clicked the keys. "Here we are. The cube with the Protocol on it was stored in the archive vault."

"I'm standing in the archive vault."

"Ah, yes. You blasted the doors and . . . let me scan the cube you found." Roach tapped a few more keys. "That's the right cube."

"As I said, Doctor. And it's blank."

"You're right. I don't understand. Unless . . ." Roach's fingers blurred over the keyboard; then he paled. "Dr. Solomon erased the contents two minutes ago."

That was what she'd been doing at the computer. At least, *part* of what she'd been doing.

"The Protocol is gone?" Hund asked.

"No. She can't have—there's an override on deletion. Wait a moment. . . ." Roach eyed the data scrolling past. "Ah! Before she erased the cube, she transferred the contents into the Holographic Hub. Into a *new* cube. We'll retrieve the Protocol from there."

"I'm on my way," Hund said, his voice crackling.

"The hub is extremely dangerous, Commander. Do not enter until I tell you it's safe."

"Roger."

"And on your way," Roach said, "kill anything that moves."

SAVED BY THE BARBIE

I could've told him that in the Holographic Hub right then, absolutely nothing was moving.

Not that I wasn't trying. I didn't remember the whole lecture my aunt had given me during that tour, about getting stuck in the hub, but the phrase *vaporize all the synapses in your brain* stuck in my mind.

And I couldn't even lift a finger.

Luckily, my face was scrunched against the computer I'd been using to send the dragonfly data to Jamie. That's what saved my life. If I'd been an inch farther away, I never would have made it. But I was close enough to hear Jamie's voice.

"Bug!" she said through the half-smashed speakers. "Bug! Can you hear me?"

I gurgled. It was all I could do.

"I can see you here, on my screen. In *CircuitBoard*, I mean. You're showing up on the game interface. What's going on?"

I tried to say, "Get me out of here!" But all I could manage was "Out!"

"You want to get out?"

I gurgled again, more insistently.

"Well, there's a . . . let's see, I'll connect the positive to the negative here, and . . ." And she was off, talking nonsense about winning her *CircuitBoard* game.

Meanwhile, my synapses were getting fried.

Jamie kept blathering about her game: "Then I close this circuit and move to the next level. I'll power down the grid, and . . ."

Everything was fading away, *fading, fading, fading, fading, fading, fading, fading, fading, fading, fading* . . .

Until I heard a click.

The humming in the room quieted and I took a sudden gulp of breath. I hadn't realized I'd stopped breathing.

"You look terrible, Doug," Jamie said through the speakers. "I'm zooming in on you. Are you okay? Can you hear me?"

I croaked, "Yes."

With the hub powered down, I felt stronger already. Then I noticed that the door was unlocked. Somehow Jamie had turned off the power and unlocked the door using *CircuitBoard* commands from her laptop.

She'd saved my life.

Talk about humiliating. Saved by a girl game.

"What on earth is going on?" Jamie asked. (But of course, she didn't put it so politely.)

"I don't know." I pushed myself onto my knees. "I gotta get out of here."

"What'd you *do*?" Jamie asked.

Then another voice came from the computer: "The Center has been taken over by mercenaries. Douglas Solomon, you must take that Memory Cube and flee."

"This one?" I asked, grabbing the cube. "Jamie? Is that you?"

"No, I—"

The mechanized voice cut her off: "You must prevent the intruders from stealing that cube. You must not fail."

"But no pressure, right?" I said.

"And you must vacate the hub," the voice said. "You have nine seconds before permanent brain damage."

"Eight."

"Seven."

"Six."

FIVE, FOUR, THREE . . .

Thirty seconds later, Hund and his soldiers closed in on the Holographic Hub. They moved like the elite mercenary commando force they were—with a deadly silence.

"Wait while I power down the hub," Roach's voice said. "It's a complex procedure and— What's this!"

"What?" Hund asked, raising his gun.

"Impossible!" Roach said over the communicator, still clicking the keyboard in the other room. "The hub's already off-line. Someone got there before us. Commander, get that cube."

Hund kicked down the door to the Holographic Hub.

He dove inside, rolled, and came up standing with a huge gun in each hand. The whole thing took him about a nanosecond.

The total time elapsed between Commander Hund's ingress into the Holographic Hub and—

Give it a rest, Auntie M, okay?

Sometimes she's a little obsessive about numbers.

If you could only see them as I see them, Douglas, you'd understand. It is one of the few advantages of my new state.

Oh. Sorry. I didn't mean to—

Apology accepted, Douglas. Please continue the story.

Okay. Commander Hund battered through the hub door, with three soldiers behind him. They fanned out and found . . . nothing but wreckage. Just the shattered furniture from my aunt's office, the scattered junk from her drawers.

Hund hit the button on his communicator. "Doctor, the Protocol cube isn't here."

Roach had left my aunt on the floor and headed for the loading bay to prepare the helicopters to transport the HostLink, because that thing was *huge*. He paused when he got Hund's message, and checked a monitor. "I'm tracking the cube in corridor 6B. No, wait. It's moving."

"Patch into the security cameras."

"One moment. Yes. Focusing. Ah! That's Dr. Solomon's brat. He spilled coleslaw on me at one of those insufferable company picnics. He has the cube. Get the Protocol and dump the body."

"My pleasure," Hund said, and started hunting me.

HAVE A NICE DAY

About a minute earlier, I'd lunged across the hub and tugged on the door handle.

"Quantum entanglement at critical levels," the voice said. "Brain waves compromised."

I recognized the mechanized tones. That was what the Center sounded like when the scientists set the output to "voice." The same bland voice said, "This is a no-entry zone," and "Download complete," and "Please fasten your seat belt."

Somehow, the Center itself was telling me that my brain waves were compromised, and in two seconds I'd have permanent brain damage. In a panic, I yanked open the door and fell into the corridor, breathing hard.

"Now hide, Douglas Solomon," the voice said. "Before they find you."

"What?" I blurted.

"Before they find the Protocol," the voice said. "Do not let them get that cube."

"But who—"

"The future is in your hands."

"How—"

"Flee now," the voice said. "Or die."

So I fled.

Down the hallway, hurdling a heap of rubble on the floor, then swerving into a stairwell with a door half blasted off its hinges. I pressed myself into the corner, holding the Memory Cube in a white-knuckled grip.

I didn't know what was going on. The explosion, falling into the hub, the threats of brain damage and prowling mercenaries—it was all too much.

They wanted this cube? For the Protocol? And I was the only person who could stop them? I mean, *me*?

I couldn't remember to take out the trash. I couldn't gather the courage to ask Stacy Nguyen to dance. I couldn't sit through an entire English class without fidgeting. And *I* was gonna keep the Protocol from a gang of mercenaries?

No.

I don't want to sound like a baby, but I needed my aunt.

So I slipped downstairs and through another door, then trotted along the corridor until I came to a console on the wall. I pressed Locate. Those things would find any authorized person in the building. Then I said, "Dr. Solomon."

"Dr. Solomon is in processing lab three," the computer voice said. "Vital signs negligible. Have a nice day."

Vital signs negligible?

I started running.

TARGET PRACTICE MAKES TARGET PERFECT

I'd never seen the processing labs—too highly classified—but I knew they were in one of the subbasements. And after that explosion had blasted the security systems, every corner of the Center was wide open.

So I took the stairs five at a time, until halfway down, a shadow fell across the landing below me.

A mercenary. I saw his uniform and his rifle, and my heart clenched.

He took a step into the stairwell. I stood there, in plain

view: I couldn't move; I couldn't think. I just . . . froze.

Let me tell you something. Maybe you have daydreams where something bad happens and you're the hero. You're smooth and quick and fearless. Maybe you foil a robber or stop a sniper attack.

The kind of thing that happens in movies and video games.

Well, in real life, you're not smooth and quick and tough; instead, your body shuts down. You think that *you* are in charge, but suddenly your legs turn into string cheese, and your brain takes a nap.

So you stand there in the open, gaping at an armed mercenary with orders to kill you on sight. You don't run or jump or plan a clever counterattack.

You just stand there.

In the open.

Like you *want* to be used for target practice.

And despite all that, despite doing everything wrong, maybe you get lucky. Maybe the merc turns without looking toward you, and heads back down the hallway on his patrol.

I slumped against the wall in relief, my head spinning and my hands shaking. Until I heard the footsteps. A dozen mercenaries thundering downstairs from above me.

That time I moved.

I darted through a door and heard someone shout, "There he is!"

I fled from the stairwell to the hallway, hearing boots pound behind me, and ran blindly through some smoldering wreckage from the explosion—just in time to see a patrol rounding the corner.

One of the mercs raised his rifle and I screamed and flung myself through a hole blasted in the opposite wall.

I tumbled into a vast cubicle farm two levels beneath the ground, as big as a football field: hundreds of cubicles, each with a computer and telephone and file cabinet.

Some had houseplants and family photos, but they *all* had cubicle dividers that transformed the room into the world's biggest maze.

I dove in like a rat.

SURROUNDED BY CATS

I can describe the next four minutes in one word: *terror.*

They stalked me through the maze, and I scurried away. I crawled around cubicles and hid beneath desks. Once, a merc stopped three feet from me, on the other side of a divider, and I heard him sniffing. Like he could *smell* me.

He started into the cubicle, and suddenly, all the phones in the room rang at the same time—and abruptly cut off.

The merc stopped, spun, and headed away.

I thought, *Saved by the bell.*

And almost laughed hysterically. Good thing I didn't, or they'd have shot me.

After a blur of fear, I found myself in a big cubicle with five workstations, crouched underneath a table holding a coffeemaker and doughnuts. Listening to the ominous silence. Waiting for them to find me, scared and alone.

Beep

Beep-beep

I trembled in my hiding spot. What was *that*?

Gurgle

The coffeemaker, set on automatic drip, had just started brewing. And making a racket: the coffeemaker was gonna lead them right to me!

I listened but didn't hear anyone close. So I crawled over to turn the coffeemaker off, and the digital display said:

DOUGLAS SOLOMON

PLEASE RESPOND

?

I huddled over the coffeemaker and whispered, "Hello?"

In a moment, the display changed.

INSUFFICIENT AUDIO

USE KEYPAD

Like everything else in the Center, the coffeemaker was pretty futuristic: the programmable keypad looked like an iPhone.

I tapped out *Here*.

I AM BLOCKING SURVEILLANCE

AND TRACKING

FOR NOW

BUT SOON THEY WILL FIND YOU

TAKE THE PROTOCOL CUBE

AND HIDE

Yeah, I got that much. Thanks for the wise advice.
I typed *Help my aunt!*

SHE IS BEYOND HELP

YOU MUST ESCAPE

"I'm not leaving without her," I whispered to the display.
Which was just great. Now I was talking to coffeepots.
I breathed and typed *How?*

MEMORIZE THIS:

BLUEPRINTS OF THE CENTER

FIND A WAY OUT

Blueprints scrolled past on the little display. Because that was me, the guy who could memorize blueprints. Sure, and I could leap tall buildings in a single bound, too.

"Are you crazy?" I muttered. Then I typed *Are you crazy?*

NEGATIVE

EXPLAIN

So I told whoever was on the other end of this coffeemaker display that I couldn't read blueprints, I couldn't do any of this. I could handle *Arsenal Five* and *Street Gang* and pizza . . . but escaping from a top secret weapons lab with mercenaries stalking me?

Not really my strength.

REFORMATTING . . .

A second later, I heard a loud hum. All around the room, printers suddenly sprang to life and spit out sheets of paper. Everywhere except in the big cubicle where I was hiding, which must've been the only place in the entire cubicle farm without a printer.

Then I heard beeping: loud at first, though getting fainter.

I AM ATTEMPTING TO LEAD THEM

AWAY

MEMORIZE THE OUTPUT OF MONITOR

NEAREST YOU

ESCAPE

WITH PROTOCOL CUBE

"Yeah, yeah," I said.

BE CAREFUL, DOUGLAS SOLOMON

NOW GO

!!!!!!!!!!!!

That was a lot of exclamation points for a coffeemaker, so I went. Well, first I checked that none of the mercenaries were nearby. Then I breathed.

Then I breathed some more.

Then I stopped trembling and stood from my hiding spot and darted across the big cubicle to the nearest monitor. I don't really know why. It wasn't like having blueprints on a bigger screen was gonna help; I still didn't know how to read them.

But if I wanted to find my aunt, I needed a map, so I checked the screen. This is what I saw:

Gingerbread muffins

2 cups flour	2 teaspoons baking soda
1 tablespoon ground ginger	1 scant teaspoon ground cinnamon
1/8 teaspoon ground cloves	1 stick salted butter
1/2 cup sugar	2 large eggs
1/2 cup light molasses	1 cup cold water

Whisk flour, baking soda, ginger, cinnamon, and cloves in a bowl.

"Gingerbread," I muttered.

"The other monitor," a mechanized voice said from the computer. "Turn clockwise approximately eighty-two degrees."

I looked both ways and saw the other computer. Then I almost smiled. Not quite, but almost, because you know what I saw on *that* screen?

The entire floor plan of the Biodigital Research Center, displayed as *Arsenal Five* levels, rotating slowly in 3-D.

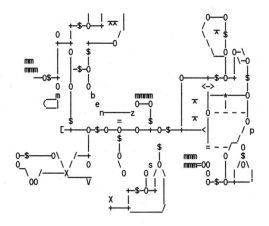

That was what the Center had meant by "reformatting"—converting the blueprints into game levels. I crouched at the computer and flicked through the five floors and the duct systems and sublevels. And let me just say one thing: I *rock* at *Arsenal Five*.

So that messy little scribble might not mean anything to you, but to me? Better than my own personal tour guide with a GPS attached.

I traced a path to an exit. The patrols were flashing red dots, and if I thought of this as a game, I knew exactly how to escape.

Probably without even losing a single life.

On second thought, I didn't want to think about how many lives I had in this game. Still, I knew I could escape, except for one thing. My aunt was in there somewhere. Processing lab three.

And I wasn't gonna leave her behind.

INTO THE FIRE

First step: get across the room and into the janitor's closet.

I crept and slithered and finally sprinted the last twenty feet into the closet and slammed the door behind me. I heard gunfire as I locked the heavy metal door.

It would take them at least three minutes to batter through that. The Center was built like a battleship.

I found the grate behind the shelves and wriggled inside—and into the next room. A bathroom. At least I emerged under the sinks, not the toilets.

Then I dashed across the hall and into processing lab one, which shared an emergency ventilation shaft with processing lab two. I dragged myself through the shaft, into PL2.

Closer and closer. One last step.

I opened the door, looked both ways down the corridor, and dashed into the open. Nobody shouted; nobody fired. I just slipped quietly into processing lab three.

Only one tiny problem: I wasn't alone.

TOO YOUNG TO DIE

I crossed into the center of the lab, surrounded by a zillion dollars in hardware. Huge brushed-aluminum sheds hummed softly on the static-resistant rubberized floor, and triple-wrapped cables wove through glowing boxes.

I found my aunt in a heap. I took five steps toward her and heard something behind me.

Commander Hund. All seven feet of muscle, weapons, and gunmetal eyes. Standing twenty feet away, staring at me.

"Figured you'd come here," he growled.

I didn't answer, didn't move. The whole "frozen in terror" thing again.

"Give me that Memory Cube, kid," Hund said. "Unless you want to join her."

He pointed at my aunt, sprawled limply on the floor, like a doll tossed to the ground.

I tried to swallow, but couldn't. I tightened my grip on the cube and focused on not fainting. And on not looking at my aunt, because I didn't want to start crying.

"Is she—" I swallowed. "Is she . . ."

"As a doornail," Hund said.

A numbness crept over me. "You killed her."

"Right now, kid," Hund said, sneering, "you oughtta worry more about who I'm gonna kill *next*."

I nodded slowly. "Yeah."

"So give."

"No."

He lifted his gun and I felt my knees weaken. I couldn't handle this. I couldn't stand up to Hund. He was too big, too scary.

And my aunt was in a heap on the ground. My aunt, who'd always been there for me—not just when my parents died, but every day, in all the little ways. She'd nagged me about chores and not about video games. She'd taught me to ride a bike, and expected me to keep trying after I'd shredded my knees. She'd driven me to the skate park and trusted that I wouldn't break my neck.

I thought about that, and I stood my ground. For her. Plus, once Hund got the cube, he'd shoot me. If I wanted to stay alive, I needed to keep that cube.

"I've got my finger on the auto-erase," I said, my voice wavering. "Anything happens to me, say good-bye to the Protocol."

"I want that data, Hund," Roach's scratchy voice said from Hund's communicator. "Now!"

I had to think. I had to clamp down on my fear, block out the sight of my aunt on the floor, and think. I replayed the *Arsenal Five* levels in my mind; if I could get out of sight for a minute, I might have a chance. Computer cables ran under the floor, in insulated ducts. Too small for Hund, but I might squeeze through the ducts from one room to the next.

"You can have the cube," I said. "Just give me a minute alone with my aunt."

Hund pulled a knife from a sheath on his leg. "You see this?"

"It's a—a knife."

"My favorite blade." He bared his teeth. "You delete the cube and I'll show you why."

Then he took a step toward me.

And another.

He was only four steps away, his knife glinting in the light.

"Give me the cube, kid."

THE SILVER LINING

At the same time my aunt died, new lives were being born. Deep in the Center's holographic patterns and artificial intelligence modules, things were happening.

Impossible things.

By definition, Douglas, nothing that happens is impossible.

Maybe so. But this was pretty close.

As you no doubt guessed, the Center used a sophisticated artificial intelligence woven through the buildings and labs and even the parking lot. The AI monitored tests and printed reports and controlled the air-conditioning and validated parking. And made coffee.

I figured it also tried to protect kids caught in mercenary attacks. I mean, obviously the mechanized voice and the coffeepot were controlled by the AI, right?

Wrong.

The first clue: the Center's AI had never been so *active* before.

Nobody wanted an artificially intelligent robotic overlord in control of a weapons lab, so they designed the AI more like a clever calculator than like Skynet. While it handled power surges and electron microscopy, it couldn't reformat the blueprints into video game levels or ring phones to distract mercenaries.

Then who did?

Well, now *that* is the question.

Minutes before Hund threatened me with his knife, a newborn Awareness swirled and clustered and slowly woke in the depths of the Center's memory system. A completely new kind of intelligence, one that didn't even have a name yet.

Just a mind, floating in the digital darkness. An offshoot of my aunt's uploaded brain—mostly—though I didn't know that then. Even *she* didn't know that then.

A sensation disturbed the quiet. The newborn Awareness scanned the area, and detected terror and panic. Internal sensors swiveled and evaluated . . . then focused on three life forms:

LARKSPUR	COSMO	POPPY

The skunks Roach had scanned into the mainframe before the detonator exploded. Their bodies had died within minutes, and their minds had dissolved into ones and zeros. But they were still afraid, still trapped inside the machine.

That was the first emotion the Awareness ever faced: the fear of three disembodied skunks. And the first emotion the Awareness ever *felt*? A combination of kindness and pity.

The Awareness realized that the skunks were on the verge of complete brain death, and with her innate sense of goodness, she refused to let innocent animals die. The Awareness scanned for output pathways, any way to return the skunks to life.

Douglas, your homework!

Gimme a minute, Auntie M. I'm getting to the good part—

Per our agreement that you'd stop posting after you revealed who was responsible for the events at the Center, I'm cutting your Net connection.

—about the bomb and the skun—

- -

TO WARN

- -

Hey, this is Jamie. Doug's got a Latin test tomorrow, and things don't look good. So he asked me to post this:

> Quick, if anyone knows how to conjugate *moneo*,
> drop me a comment.
> *Moneo, monere* . . . what?

Monici? Monicatum? Monkeyficium?

Sheesh. If Latin weren't already a dead language,
I'd kill it myself. Also, if you know the answers to
exercitia nine through eleven in the study guide—

CONNECTION TERMINATED

BALANCED ON A KNIFE EDGE

Sorry I haven't posted in a few days. Well, a few weeks. Okay,
a month.

Things got a little crazy around here between the cyberdroid attack on Wall Street and my getting a 71 percent on my
Latin test. Oh, you thought the stock market just crashed for
no reason? No, that was Roach and VIRUS.

And Aunt Margaret made me sign up for this after-school
project that'll raise my grade to a solid B-minus. A play for
Latin class. I don't want to talk about it.

You make an admirable Hermes, Douglas.

I wear a dress in school. Not really helping my social life.

That's not a dress; that's a toga.

What part of "I don't want to talk about it" did you not
understand?

Apologies, Douglas.

The thing is, fighting VIRUS is more important than

schoolwork, but my aunt insists that a B average is part of my cover. Just an ordinary student, blending into the crowd.

So I'm sorry about the long silence on the blog. And yeah, I'm talking to you, MealyMouth13, the only guy who left a comment. I'll overlook the fact that all you said was "ur r teh suxxor! more C'/BEr§kuNkz!!!"

Anyway, for all you lurkers, don't worry. Auntie M's been monitoring the hits, making sure that Roach can't trace them. Can't trace *you*.

But if things are so busy, why am I back?

I mean, I've still got no proof that I didn't kill my aunt. I've still got no proof of *any* of this—at least, none that I can safely share.

I'm back because I can't be the only one who knows what's happening. They say the truth is out there. Well, it's my job to make sure they're right. This information is too important to lose.

Also, I'm stuck on level twenty-nine of *Ambush Z*. Can someone throw me a bone?

YOU ARE HERE

So my last post about the Center ended with me in processing lab three, my lifeless aunt on the floor and Commander Hund stalking forward with his blade drawn.

"Take your finger off the cube, kid," Hund said.

I gaped at his knife. "If I do, you'll k-kill me."

"Maybe I'll let you go," he said.

"But you w-won't."

His smile made me shiver. "Give me the cube, and you won't feel a thing."

The sad truth is he scared me so much I almost did what he said. Then I remembered my aunt and shook my head. "I'll erase it."

And into the silence, Roach's voice came: "Commander Hund, I just finished checking, and there *is* no auto-erase on that cube."

Hund laughed horribly. "You're bluffing me? Bad decision."

He spun the knife in his hand and stepped closer

a
n
d

c
l
o
s
e
r

until he plucked the cube from my hand.

Well, so much for that. So much for *me*. After everything that had happened, I'd lost the Protocol.

I'd had only one job: to keep the Protocol safe. Now I'd failed. I'd lost my aunt and I'd failed.

And my problems were just beginning.

Hund slid the cube into his pocket and drew his arm back to slash me with the knife—and the lights went out.

A voice yelled, "Hund!" from across the room, and he reacted, quick as thought. Guns suddenly in his hands, he pivoted, sidestepping into the darkness, completely silent. Stalking whatever had called his name.

His implanted lens shimmered briefly, then turned black in the gloom.

Night vision.

A footstep sounded behind a huge electron microscope, and Hund murmured into his communicator. "Roach. There's an intruder in processing lab three."

"Scanning," Roach's voice said. "One moment."

Hund slipped like a shadow around the scope and I heard my aunt whisper, "Doug, get out. Now."

I looked down. My aunt was on the floor. Her eyes were closed. Her lips were not moving; she wasn't breathing. She sure wasn't whispering. I swallowed the lump in my throat and blinked back tears.

"Now!" her voice repeated. "Slow and steady, don't attract his attention. . . ."

I started backing toward the door, wiping my eyes with the heel of my hand.

When I got halfway to the corridor, I heard Roach's voice: "Nothing there. Only audio inference. Get that cube."

"Already got it," Hund grunted. "And now for the boy."

"The explosion will take care of him."

My breath caught. *Explosion? What explosion?*

"The little twerp tried to *bluff* me," Hund growled. "This is personal."

That snapped me out of my fear and grief. I shot the rest of the way across the room and sprinted into the corridor.

FASTER, STRONGER, BIGGER

I heard Hund behind me. He was a trained mercenary killer, and I was a kid. He was faster than me, stronger than me, bigger than me. There was no chance I was going to get away.

Still, I ran as fast as I could. Out the door, down the hall. I scrambled around the wreckage, waiting for the gunshot.

Then something tugged at my mind. What was it? He was *faster*. No. He was *stronger*. Obviously. He was *bigger* . . .

That was it—bigger!

I charged past two doors, grabbed the handle of the third, and spun inside, hearing Hund's boots close behind me.

I didn't hesitate. I had no idea what this room was for, but I'd seen it on the *Arsenal Five* blueprints, and I figured—

The room to which you refer housed the data-compression modules.

Would you stop interrupting? I'm trying to tell a story here. Do the words *dramatic tension* mean nothing to you?

Anyway, inside the room, an array of huge modules extended from the floor to the ceiling, each about six feet square with maybe a foot between them. I could just squeeze into the gaps. No way a guy Hund's size could follow.

I squeezed, as fast as I could, then moved down five rows, losing myself in the maze. . . .

I heard Hund step into the room. "Nice try, kid," he called. "But the exterminator doesn't need to crawl into the rat hole."

I heard a *pfffft*. A second later, something clanked to the ground.

"That's tear gas," Hund said. "You're gonna learn a lesson in pain."

Even though the canister landed on the other side of a module, I could already smell the gas. I looked around, desperate for a way out. My eyes started watering again, not only because I'd lost my aunt, but also because of the tear gas in the air.

Then I found what I was looking for. On the floor was an access grate leading to a cable duct. My eyes stung, and I couldn't stop blinking, but I managed to pull the grate open and felt the breeze of the ventilation system that cooled the wires.

"I've got a mask for you right here," Hund said. "Come out and I'll make everything all right."

Yeah, I bet you will, I thought.

The tear gas burned my nose and throat and eyes, and I could barely see. But I didn't need to see to follow the breeze and squeeze under the floor into the duct.

A BALL OF FAIL

I closed the grate overhead and squirmed away. The duct was maybe two inches wider than my shoulders. I groped blindly ahead—twenty feet, fifty feet—until my heartbeat returned to normal and my vision cleared. Then I lay back in the darkness under an unknown room and just . . . stopped.

I didn't know where to go. I didn't know what to do. I didn't want to think about Roach or Hund or the Protocol cube—or my aunt, lying limp on the floor.

All I wanted was to curl into a ball and forget.

WHAT, NO ICE MAKER?

After a while, voices drifted through the floor above my head. A man and a woman were talking—a pair of Hund's mercenaries.

"You done with this room?" the woman asked.

The man grunted. "One more crate."

"What *is* all this stuff?"

"HostLink accessories." The crate clattered, and the man grunted again. "They want this lab packed up."

I squirmed in the cramped duct, worming my way closer to a hatch, where I peeked into the room overhead. I saw a sliver of a research lab with black counters and futuristic science gear. The mercenaries were loading everything onto a cart, stealing every last scrap of technology and data . . . or *almost* every last scrap.

"What're we supposed to do with that?" the man asked, gesturing to this . . . *thing* in the corner that looked like a refrigerator covered with snakeskin. "It won't fit on the cart."

"Our orders are to take everything we can. They'll destroy the rest."

"Another bomb?"

The woman grinned coldly. "A small-yield nuke. The commander likes his explosions."

"Let's haul, then. Don't wanna get left behind with *that* going off."

"No worries. We're almost done. C'mon."

They rattled away, and I shifted uncomfortably in the duct. When you're inside one, a cable duct feels an awful lot like a coffin. Especially when you just saw your aunt sprawled on the floor and the words *small-yield nuke* got dropped into the conversation. So as soon as the sound of the cart faded, I climbed into the room.

Where something whispered, "Sug."

I yelped—but softly.

"Sug Solomon. Ssep a lissle sloser."

Step a little closer? I turned slowly and eyed the fridge-thing. The snakeskin was coated with what looked like barnacles.

"Yes, here." The barnacles opened and closed, making the eerie whispering. "San you hear? There is no visual abilisy."

I kept my distance. "Um, who are you?"

"Lise the soffeemaser."

"The coffeemaker?"

"Yes. Lissen, Sug—"

"First a coffeemaker, and now I'm talking to a snake fridge?" I said. "With barnacles?"

"Lissen! You muss fin—"

"I lost the Protocol cube."

"I know. We muss—"

Well, let me translate. A little of that snake fridge accent goes a long way.

Fridge: We must fight Roach.

Me: You and me? Against *them*? You're a big snakeskin box.

Fridge: I am not this structure. I am a new function of the Center's AI. This "snakeskin box" is merely a storage container I am using to communicate. We need the Protocol.

Me: I lost the Protocol.

Fridge: There is another copy, one Roach doesn't know about. We can only beat him if we have our own Protocol. Otherwise, he will scan in millions of innocent people and—

Me: So stop whispering and get the Protocol! Oh, and they're setting off a bomb. A nuke.

Fridge: The copy is not yet encoded into wetware.

Me: A nuke, a nuke! They're setting off a *nuke*!

Fridge: Then you must hurry.

A SHORT BREAK FOR A BRIEF MELTDOWN

Instead of hurrying, I panicked. My breath grew shallow, and my knees turned to applesauce.

And I suddenly, desperately wished I'd known my mom

better—because I wanted to pray for her to help me. If ever I needed someone watching from above, that time was now.

I knew that Auntie M would watch over me if she could, but I couldn't accept that she was dead. I still expected her to walk through the door and make everything all right—even though I knew that wasn't possible.

I started to hyperventilate, my mind spinning in crazy circles.

Then a thought struck me: maybe Auntie M wasn't gonna walk through the door, but she'd made me who I was. And maybe I'd never known my mom, but that didn't matter. Not at all. Because if she was watching, *she* knew *me*.

I took a few deep breaths. *This one's for you, Auntie M. And for you, Mom.*

CHILLING LIKE A VILLAIN

Fridge: Better now?

Me: Tell me what I need to do.

Fridge: I will download a copy of the Protocol into a biodigital format—three test skunks currently in a digitized state.

Me: You're gonna download the Protocol into *skunks*?

Fridge: Yes. Inside this "snakeskin box," you will
find modified stem-cell self-extraction
media.

Me: Are you kidding? I'll find *what*?

Fridge: Objects the approximate size and texture
of T-bone steaks. Take them to workshop
seven.

Me: Where's that?

Fridge: I will print a map. Inside workshop seven,
you will find the HostLink prototype,
and—

Me: Would you stop with the crazy names?
The GhostLink?

Fridge: HostLink. The next generation of uplinks.
The only way to transfer millions of minds
into data files at once. Advanced beyond
anything—

Me: Fine, a HostLink. What does it look like?

Fridge: The word *HostLink* is printed on the
side. Insert the "steaks," and initiate six
thousand iterations—

Me: Wait! Stop! Gimme the kiddie version.

Fridge: Plug the steaks into the HostLink. They
will adapt to any port. I will transfer the
Protocol, and the HostLink will output the

steaks as the skunks' bodies. Then you
will take the animals home and find a way
to extract the Protocol.

Me: So I take some steaks from inside this
snake fridge and plug them into a machine
in workshop seven? They'll turn into
skunks. Then I take the skunks home?

Fridge: Yes.

Me: Why didn't you just say that?

Fridge: Do not fail this time. If you don't get the
Protocol, nothing can stop Roach.

COMPLETELY 10010000

I looked for a door handle on the snakeskin fridge. I looked
for a latch. Instead, I found a seam inside a flap of skin. Like
a puckered scar. It was oozing neon green glop.

"Reach inside," the fridge whispered.

So I wormed my hand to the inside, which was slimy and
warm and throbbing faintly.

Dis. Gusting.

"Deeper," the fridge said. "Until your elbow is at the seam."

So I shoved my hand in deeper, until my elbow disappeared into the seam. And my fingertips felt . . . something.

Something harder and more distinct than warm humming goo.

I hooked an edge with my fingers and pulled against the resistance of the glop inside. Then another edge, and another. Finally, with a wet *splooch*, I dragged three meaty chunks through the seam.

And they did look kinda like T-bone steaks, except with touch screens and stubby little plugs—which might've been cool if I hadn't been covered in snakeskin-fridge goo.

- -

AND NOW, A WORD FROM OUR SPONSOR

- -

Hey. This is Jamie. I'm posting this a couple of months after the Center exploded, and a couple thousand miles away. And with the benefit of hindsight.

This whole story is about to get so crazy—well, so much crazi*er*—that I told Doug he should explain some things.

He said, "If you think it's a problem, you do it."

He's such a bug sometimes.

Anyway, to give you some background, let me start with myself: your classic case of "poor little rich girl." My parents were—*are*—both lawyers. They made a lot of money, but they worked seventy hours a week and spent another ten driving back and forth to their offices in the city.

I had everything, kinda. They loved me, they provided for me—but they were never really *there* for me. Unlike Doug's aunt.

So I used to act out a little, and . . . Let's just say that I've been to my share of therapists. I'm over all that, though. Mostly thanks to Dr. Solomon. After Bug and I became friends, she really took me under her wing. She's sort of my hero. She said I've got the mind for science, too, which is all I've ever wanted.

Enough of my personal Hallmark Moment.

What I want to explain is this:

First, those test skunks were digitized. Their bodies died, and they existed only as digital information.

Then there's the new Awareness that Bug mentioned. We had no clue what was happening in the Center's data banks at the time, of course. But that Awareness spawned from Dr. Solomon's scanned mind, then merged with the Center's AI, forming a brand-new identity. And that Awareness grafted a backup copy of the Protocol, which Roach didn't know about, onto the skunks. So three digital skunks contained the most powerful cybernautic code on the planet.

But their minds were stuck in the machine. The output paths were destroyed.

Soon they'd die, too.

That's what those "steaks" were: a way to output scanned minds into physical bodies. Kind of like clay that you can sculpt into any shape. Because when you transfer a digital entity to the real world, you need *something* from which the body can grow. Well, usually.

So once the Center gave the right commands, the "steaks" would grow back into real skunks—into Larkspur, Cosmo, and Poppy.

Except *now* they'd contain the Protocol.

Only one catch: for precision work like that, to re-create the test skunks exactly, you needed the HostLink in workshop seven. Otherwise, things could get *craaaazy.*

CHAMBER OF HORRORS

Me again. Doug. While I was getting those techno-steaks, *this* conversation was happening across the Center:

"Commander Hund," Roach said, tapping at a wall-display keyboard, "I've intercepted a communication to the boy."

Hund turned from the door. "Where is he?"

"Heading for workshop seven—just like you." Roach touched a few more keys. "There! I finished prepping the HostLink for transport. You're clear. Remove it before the boy arrives."

"I'll wait until he shows," Hund said. "Then I'll remove him, too."

"He's not important, but the HostLink is critical."

"I can grab the machine *and* kill the boy."

Roach smiled coldly. "I'll send my little pet after the Solomon brat. You get the equipment. Now go."

Hund turned on his heel and prowled away.

To workshop seven.

THE LONELIEST NUMBER

I stuffed the three steaks into a specimen pack I found on the floor, and turned back toward the fridge-thing. "Anything else?"

"Roach is destroying all the data banks he can't steal," it said. "I will not remain coherent much longer. You are on your own."

"Great."

"I believe," the thing whispered, "in you."

I grabbed the map that spewed from a nearby printer, and the countdown started. A calm computerized voice came from all the speakers: "Self-destruct initiated. Detonation sequence in forty minutes. Self-destruct initiated. Detonation sequence in forty minutes. Self-destruct initiated. Detonation sequence in forty minutes. Self-destruct sequence initiated. Detonation sequence in forty minutes. Self-destruct initiated. Detonation sequence in forty minutes. Self-destruct initiated. Detonation sequence in forty minutes. Self-destruct initiated. Detonation sequence in forty minutes. Self-destruct sequence initiated.

HE COULD'VE JUST ADOPTED A HAMSTER

By the time the message changed to "Detonation sequence in *thirty-nine* minutes," I'd raced along two corridors and bounded down three flights of stairs.

If I correctly remembered the floor plan the coffeemaker had shown me, about fifty soldiers patrolled the Center, in groups of two. Except I guessed they weren't patrolling, not anymore. Now they were looting—dragging all the HostLink components to the loading dock.

So aside from the random patrol, I didn't have anything to worry about.

Well, other than Hund.

And the tactical nuke.

And the Protocol.

And my aunt.

But other than all *that*? Clear sailing.

Or so I thought, until I stepped from a stairwell in one of the lower sublevels and froze.

Something was slithering toward me from a hole in the wall. A snake or a tentacle or a . . . I didn't know. I didn't stick around to find out. I scrambled backward, and the thing emerged with a *thhhht* from the crack.

It was a centipede about the size of my leg, with a sequence of lights flashing inside and two antennae quivering from each armored segment. All of them waved at me as the thing undulated closer. It wove between the stair railings, then slithered along the wall, and I saw that it crept on tractor treads layered with tiny suction cups instead of a thousand legs.

This time, I didn't freeze in terror. I backpedaled upstairs as the thing slithered toward me, fiber-optic antennae waving.

I waited—two seconds, three seconds—then put my hand on the stair railing and vaulted.

I spun in the air, the specimen pack containing the steaks flopping at my side, and landed in a crouch on the landing below. Behind me, I heard the centipede drop from the wall to the floor and scrabble toward the edge of the stairs, ready to leap onto my head and shove pincers into my eyes.

Well, at least I *thought* that was what it wanted.

I shot into the hallway, then closed and bolted the door to the stairway. Much better. I checked the map. Only a few hallways, a tunnel, and an access shaft remained between me and workshop seven.

I crept down a hallway.

I crept down another hallway.

I crept down a third hallway.

And I froze when I heard voices. Sounded like mercenaries grumbling about the helicopter transport. Coming from a big echoing room down the corridor, with a huge monitor and tiers of plush seats.

An auditorium or a surgical theater: an operating room with a view.

I paused outside the door. The voices sounded distant and . . . *fuzzy*, somehow. Staticky. Then I realized I wasn't hearing the mercenaries themselves, just their voices broadcast in the room. Like someone had left a walkie-talkie on one of the seats.

I slumped in relief, took a single step forward, then saw what was broadcasting the voices. And believe me, it was no walkie-talkie.

Instead, I found myself staring at my first cyborg monster.

Imagine the body of an orangutan, squat and muscular with long arms. Now replace the fur with elephant skin—except as slimy as a slug's foot—and the hands with knobby paddles.

And instead of a head, picture a helmet: a glowing dome, like an upside-down punchbowl with an oil slick swirling in it.

Roach's "little pet." A monkeybeast.

One of the first generation of biodroids, though I didn't know that yet. A crude version, because Roach didn't have the Protocol . . . but still dangerous. Still deadly.

Most of the creatures—or machines or whatever—built by the Center were made for scientific applications. Like that snakeskin fridge, or even, I guess, that fiber-optic centipede, which—

That was one of my designs. An experimental

emergency medical unit for disaster response. A mobile, self-guided medic with nanotech healing capacity.

Yeah, I got that. Especially the "experimental" part.

Anyway, *Roach's* biodroids were made for one thing and one thing only: destruction.

I stared at the monkeybeast, holding my breath. Afraid to move, even though it was facing the opposite direction.

Then, with one last crackle of static, the voices stopped. A gear whined and the shimmer of the biodroid's helmet intensified. Its arms shifted unnaturally and seemed to break backward. A second later, its legs did the same.

Suddenly, the thing *was* facing me.

A bony knob on its shoulder swiveled and throbbed; then its legs tensed and the monkeybeast leapt from chair to chair—right toward me!

I slammed the door and ran, but a second later, the thing smashed through and skidded across the hall to the opposite wall. The biodroid wasted a few seconds stomping the wreckage of the door into smaller bits of wreckage—nasty temper. Then it turned toward me, and a stubby gun barrel slid from its armpit.

I dodged behind a snack machine, and the monkeybeast blasted a hole in concrete wall down the corridor.

Looking around, I saw . . . nothing. No way out. Just a long hallway with a few doors at one end and a snack machine in the middle.

And a monkeybeast, stalking closer for the kill.

For the record, Douglas, the machine to which you are referring did not vend snacks.

Looked like a snack machine to me.

That particular model dispensed preprogrammed nutrient media for the researchers, for propagation of—

Whatever. I'm pretty sure I saw potato chips.

Anyway, the vending machine didn't offer much cover. And once the biodroid stepped closer, the machine offered no cover at all.

Just me and a monkeybeast, five feet apart. The gun muzzle swiveled, aiming at my forehead.

Killed by an armpit gun. What a way to go.

I closed my eyes and waited for the end.

THE CREEPING DOOM

Then I heard something.

A scrabbling. A *pok! Pok-pok! Bzzzzt—thwing!*

I opened one eye and saw the biodroid reeling backward, swaying and stumbling and beating itself on the face and neck. It was trying to dislodge the centipede draped across its head, five fiber-optic antennae wriggling madly, trying to burrow into the droid.

I understood in a flash that the centipede had been trying to protect me, to save me from the monkeybeast. It hadn't been trying to *eat* me; it had been trying to *herd* me.

Well, I can take a hint.

I stood and ran. The sounds of the fight—crashing and pounding and an electric zapping—followed me around the corner and through the double doors. As I fled, I frantically consulted the map from the snake-fridge room that had been helpfully translated into *Arsenal Five* levels.

I saw the route in a flash and shoved through swinging doors into a small medical bay. In the corner, I crawled under a storage cabinet to an unlocked grate on the floor. I squeezed through and wormed my way along a vent until I fell into a conference room in the particle accelerator wing. I raced down the hall into a lab and pushed into the air lock.

Then I waited for the far side of the air lock to open. Seconds ticked by. The countdown continued. A screen on the wall flashed information about the BattleArmor development lab and the virtual reality combat simulators.

I read it as I waited for the door to unseal, shifting my weight from my left foot to my right. I'd never heard of the BattleArmor or the combat sim before then and thought they didn't matter.

Wrong again.

I muttered, "C'mon, open!" as I read, and finally the air lock door unsealed.

Then I trotted along the doughnut-shaped tunnel, counting the manhole covers—made from some shimmering plastic alloy—as I ran: one, two, three, four, five, six . . .

At the seventh, I knelt and yanked at the cool smooth handles and my vision started to darken. I felt dizzy and light-headed and

the world

swirled

and I fell on my butt, breathing hard.

What was *that*?

It felt worse than panic, worse than exhaustion.

I remembered what the Center's voice had said: *Brain waves compromised.* Were dizzy spells some aftereffect of getting stuck in the Holographic Hub? Just what I needed right then.

Luckily, when I shook my head, my vision cleared. So I finished tugging at the manhole cover, and with a *shhhh* of depressurization, the seal broke.

I slipped through and found myself in a vertical shaft.

ANFSCD

I climbed down the ladder—three stories underground—then stopped at the access hatch. Workshop seven was just around the corner.

Only one problem: the hatch was secured with a complex electronic lock with a card-swipe, retinal scanner, and keypad.

I slumped in defeat, completely baffled.

Then I got the glimmering of an idea. A bad idea, but not worse than letting Roach steal the only copy of the Protocol. Not worse than failing to download another copy that could be used against him. And *definitely* not worse than being locked inside the Center when a nuke exploded.

So I tapped *707* on the keypad. I waited a second, then tapped *7070707*.

Then:

7077077077077077077077077077077707
7077077077077077077077077077077707
707707707707707707707707707707707
707707707707707707707707707707707

Because whenever I text, *707* means SOS. And I really, really needed help.

Then I waited. And waited. Yet nobody answered.

Well, unless you count the announcement in the distance: "Self-destruct initiated. Detonation sequence in thirty-four minutes. Self-destruct initiated. Detonation sequence in thirty-four minutes."

Then the keypad beeped twice, and I looked more closely. Three letters flashed at me: *BUG?*

I tapped in **JJ!** (I called Jamie JJ online.)

Jamie: **RUIT?** (Are you in trouble?)

Well, I didn't want to say too much, in case Roach was somehow monitoring the conversation. Fortunately, Jamie and I texted enough that we used the same shorthand. And even more fortunately, she was using her newly supercharged laptop, with a direct link to the Holographic Hub, which monitored the entire Center.

I'll explain about her laptop later—but right then, the important thing was that my desperate call for help had popped onto her screen.

I thought for a second, then entered *EMRTW*. (Evil Monkeys Rule the World. Telling her I was in trouble.)

Jamie: **WUN?** (What do you need?)

Me: **FRED.** (Friggin' Ridiculous Electronic Device.)

Jamie: **LB4?** (Like before?)

Me: **ATSL.** (Along the Same Lines.)

Jamie: **. . .**

Me (frantically): **OPNTHELOKINEDU2OPEN HATCH!**

Jamie: **UNLOCK?**

Me: **Y.** (Yesssssssssssssssssssss!)

Jamie: **UNTCO.** (You Need to Chill Out.)

Me (hyperventilating): **STPPYNOZGTW!** (Stop picking your nose, get to work!)

Ten seconds later . . .

The access hatch: *Shhhhhht.*

Unlocked!

Me: **UROCK.**

Jamie: **LYLAB.**

Me: **LYLAS.**

Love You Like a Brother. Love You Like a Sister.

HAPPY BIRTHDAY TO ME

Long story short: I found workshop seven around the corner.

Hiding behind a janitorial cart, I eased closer and closer, then stopped, ten feet outside the room. Just in time to watch Roach's men wheeling this huge pod into the service elevator.

And on the side of the pod, in big letters:

HOSTLINK

I'd arrived too late. Instead of downloading the Protocol into the three cloned skunks, here's what I'd achieved: I'd moved a few steaks around.

Perfect. We needed a hero, and we got a T-bone delivery boy.

To make matters worse, Commander Hund loomed inside the freight elevator, his implanted eye scanning the corridor as the soldiers loaded more crates.

He tapped his communicator and said, "HostLink secured. Bring us up."

"Excellent," Roach replied. "With the Protocol and the HostLink, we cannot conceivably be defeated."

"The boy—"

"Ignore him. In twenty-five minutes, he'll be vaporized."

"He's right in front of me," Hund said, looking at the janitorial cart. "He thinks he's hiding."

"Then kill him, what do I care? Just don't delay!"

Hund pulled his guns and blasted away, not even aiming for me, just shredding the cart. Floor wax and glass cleaner splashed everywhere, and I was exposed, crouched in the middle of the hall.

Hund bared his teeth. "Should I wait twenty-five minutes—or put you out of your misery right now?"

I shook my head.

"Your wish is my command," he said as the elevator doors started closing. "But here's a parting gift."

Then he shot me.

EXCRUCIATING

In my calf.

A terrible burning pain.

Agony.

I curled into a tight ball. Maybe I screamed.

PAGING DR. MANDIBLE

Something hissed and popped and crawled toward me—the centipede, looking pretty rough. Charred and cracked and missing half its segments.

Two of its antennae probed the bullet hole—and in about five seconds, the pain turned to numbness. I blinked the tears from my eyes. My heartbeat slowed a little. My breath stopped coming in short harsh gasps. And a minute after that, the centipede finished sewing the hole in my leg closed.

"Um, thanks," I squeaked.

The centipede reared back and sprayed a clear adhesive patch on the wound. A cool sensation penetrated my skin, and the scent of eucalyptus mixed with the lingering stench of melted plastic and gunpowder.

"Are you the AI?" I asked, suddenly calm. Probably from a sedative in that spray. "Can you talk?"

Three of the centipede's segments cocked, almost quizzically. Then, with a sudden *ttz-pop*, it keeled over. The tractor treads on the underside spun momentarily, then stopped as a cloud of black smoke belched forth.

I don't know what was in that painkiller, but I patted the centipede on the head and stood. My leg didn't hurt; I wasn't even limping. And my mind was clear.

I pored over the map. For the first time, I knew exactly what to do.

RAGING BLUE

"Self-destruct initiated. Detonation sequence in twenty-four minutes. Self-destruct initiated. Detonation sequence in twenty-four minutes."

Twenty-four minutes. Plenty of time.

I grabbed the specimen pack with the steaks and ran. Corridor to vent shaft to access ladder. Supply depot to executive washroom to hallway.

And from the hallway to the BattleArmor development

lab, a big square room with equipment and paperwork strewn everywhere in the aftermath of the explosion. But the blast hadn't even scratched the prototype Quantuum 19 BattleArmor.

At that time, I didn't know anything about the BattleArmor other than the name, which I'd read on the screen inside the air lock. Well, and the fact that nobody ever got the prototype working right. I didn't care about that. I was just looking for places to plug in the steaks. The massive ilatfanium-alloy suit loomed in the corner of the room, with thick cables snaking around plates of impenetrable armor, from gauntlets to a half mask.

I darted to the console beside the BattleArmor, then stopped, eyeing the dozens of switches. No idea how to do this. So I flipped every switch and spoke into the console. "If you can hear me, get ready. Steak's on."

I plugged one of the steaks into a port on the prototype and nothing happened. So I popped the safety cap beside the port and pressed the button.

Nothing continued to happen.

Huh.

I gave the console a good whack.

Still nothing.

"That's just great," I muttered.

I didn't really care when kilns exploded or streetlights

flickered—and fine, people called me Bug—but this was a bad time for my technology curse to kick in.

I just shook my head and crossed toward the door. I had one more chance, if I remembered the information on that air lock screen right. Maybe not as good as the BattleArmor, but I wasn't about to quit now.

Halfway across the room, I heard a sudden humming. I turned and saw the steak pulsing and glowing a faint blue at the BattleArmor port.

"That's more like it," I said.

Then the steak turned brighter. And brighter. And hotter. Until some papers on the floor caught fire, and plastic started melting off computers and cables, and a fire alarm sounded.

The steak streamed inside the suit through the port, growing bigger and hotter and brighter until I had to look away.

The heat forced me into the hallway, and a moment before I slammed the door, the entire lab burst into a raging blue fire.

TAKE TWO

Well. *That* hadn't gone as planned.

Not that I really had a plan. Still, I'd hoped for something more constructive than setting the place on fire.

No time to worry, though. Instead, I'd check the map and start Plan B.

"Self-destruct initiated. Detonation sequence in nineteen minutes. Self-destruct initiated. Detonation sequence in nineteen minutes."

On the same floor, in the same corridor, I found the virtual reality combat simulator. The sim looked like the cockpit of a jet fighter, with a scuba suit in the pilot's seat. Apparently, a trainee—or "test subject," maybe—would zip into the scuba suit, and they'd run whichever simulation they wanted, with feedback delivered through the suit.

Urban warfare, demolitions, unarmed combat, the works.

But, I learned later, the simulations were *too* good and sometimes actually injured trainees with virtual wounds. So they'd set the simulator to Nonlethal, for safety.

After a minute of furious searching, I found a port at the bottom of the machine, then plugged in the steak and flipped the switches.

This time, the reaction was immediate. Not fire:

SPARKS

Tiny bursts of electricity zapped off the steak, stinging my fingers, then arcing into the cockpit of the VR simulator. I heard an ominous sizzle as the bursts started spraying around the room. A zigzag blast of lightning fried the potted plant beside me, and I ran, only one step ahead of the chain lightning.

HIGH SCORE

With one last steak in the specimen pack, I'd run out of ideas.

"Self-destruct initiated. Detonation sequence in fourteen minutes. Self-destruct initiated. Detonation sequence in fourteen minutes."

Fourteen minutes. Not enough time to get away. With the Center's AI off-line, I couldn't expect any help, and I didn't have any clue where to plug in the last steak.

So I figured, what the heck?

Might as well die with a smile on my face.

In the employee lounge, I started a game of *Street Gang*, the Hog Stompers versus the Fists of Kung Fu, as the Center crashed and burned around me.

On a lark, I plugged the cable of the last steak into the game port. I mean, why not?

Maybe it would help me beat my high score.

SIX THOUSAND ITERATIONS

Hey, this is Jamie again.

A few things you need to know:

First, I've seen all Dr. Solomon's digital reconstructions, and that didn't look anything like a fridge.

Second, those stem seeds—the "steaks"—were designed to work in the HostLink, right? To put the skunk minds, for example, back into their ordinary skunk bodies. But with an emergency override, they'd activate around *any* sufficient amount of technology. So Doug, for once, had the right idea—as long as you were willing to accept some uncontrollable chaos.

And by *chaos,* I mean *insanity.*

One more thing: Do you know the difference between digital information and physical *stuff* at the subatomic level? Between a software program and an elephant? Between a million lines of code and a strawberry smoothie?

Nothing. If you look closely enough, there's no difference at all. Life emerges from things that aren't alive. From molecules, from atoms, from quarks, from membranes vibrating in sixteen-dimensional space.

    Bug: **BORING, JJ . . .**
    damselfly: **WHAT NOW?**

Bug: **NOBODY WANTS TO READ ABOUT SIXTEEN-DIMENSIONAL SPACE.**

damselfly: **HEY, I DIDN'T INTERRUPT WHEN YOU WERE GETTING BORING.**

Bug: **YOU'VE BEEN IMING COMPLAINTS THIS WHOLE TIME!**

damselfly: **ONLY BECAUSE YOU DON'T KNOW THE DIFFERENCE BETWEEN ITS AND IT'S.**

Bug: **I DO TOO.**

damselfly: **THEN WHAT'S THE DIFFERENCE?**

Bug: **THE DIFFERENCE IS, SHUT UP. AND STOP TALKING ABOUT QUARKS AND MOLECULES.**

damselfly: **FINE.**

Bug: **JUST TELL THEM WHAT THEY NEED TO KNOW.**

damselfly: **FINE.**

Bug: **FINE.**

damselfly: **FINE.**

Sorry about that. Try to ignore the trolls.

In any case, at the subatomic level, everything is made of the same stuff. *Everything*. And with the Protocol and the stem seeds, you could translate digital information to physical reality and back again.

A chunk of "steak" could unzip into a polar bear or a toaster oven, then vanish into a flash of electrons and stream into a computer as pure software.

You know exactly where this is going, don't you?

Start with the BattleArmor, the combat simulator, and the video game. Add the new Awareness that Bug mentioned, which had been hiding, waiting, watching—and which overrode the normal safeguards to output the three skunks.

Larkspur: routed through the Quantuum 19 BattleArmor.

Cosmo: routed through the virtual reality combat simulator.

Poppy: routed through the *Street Gang* video game.

A walking tank, an elite commando, and a kung fu biker chick.

Yeah, and skunks.

Except not *entirely* skunks.

Remember back when that "snake fridge" told Doug about "six thousand iterations"? That just means doing something six thousand times, like running a test over and over, or pressing Next six thousand times in a row.

And the skunks had lived and learned and evolved through millions of iterations, drawing on the knowledge of the Center, on databases of human biology and old movies and joke-a-day calendars and—

Wait. How'd I get stuck with the boring explanations again?

Doug here.

As the countdown continued, I pounded on the Fire button, and on the video screen, my Hog Stomper swung his motorcycle twice around his head and—

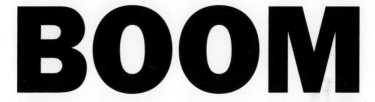

The game exploded. But not in fire or lightning or shrapnel; that would've killed me.

No, it was an explosion of goo, of flesh. Of . . . steak.

Strictly speaking, Douglas, you were impacted by self-extracting nanocellular matter, not flesh. Flesh is the soft tissue of the body of a vertebrate, whereas—

Marshmallow, then.

Imagine an 18-wheeler made of marshmallow hitting you at sixty miles an hour. Apparently, plugging that steak into the video game made it available to the new Awareness, which was searching for ways to output the skunks.

The bad news: I got slammed across the room while the speakers broadcast, "Self-destruct initiated. Detonation sequence in nine minutes."

The good news: because I hooked the steak up to Street Fighter, the Awareness was able to output Poppy.

When my vision returned, I stared at the video machines, which were now completely engulfed by a bubbling mound of goop. Then I looked higher, toward the ceiling.

At the digital announcement banner.

```
UBSECTOR 2W . . . GO TO THE ROOT
CANAL . . . CATCH THE BLUE SHUTTLE
IN SUBSECTOR 2W . . . GO TO THE ROOT
CANAL . . . CATCH THE BLUE SHUTTLE
IN SUBSECTOR 2W . . . GO TO THE ROOT
CANAL . . . CATCH THE BLUE SHUTTLE
IN SUBSECTOR 2W . . . GO TO THE ROOT
CANAL . . . CATCH THE BLUE SHUTTLE
```

"Um," I said. "Me?"

"Self-destruct initiated," the speakers answered. "Detonation sequence in eight minutes."

"Yeah," I said, looking at my map.

Catch the blue shuttle in subsector 2W? Why not? It's not like I had other plans.

WELL, *MY* MIDDLE NAME IS JOHN

Five minutes later, inside the loading dock, Hund told his soldiers, "If you so much as scratch that thing, you answer to me."

The guys operating the crane and forklift paled slightly, then *verrrrry* carefully lowered the huge pod—the one with *HOSTLINK* written on the side—onto the transport pallet.

"That's the last load," Hund said.

Across the loading dock, Roach tapped the Protocol cube, his eyes shining with glee. "Combine this Protocol with the HostLink, and the country is ours. Not in a decade, not in a year. Not even in months. In weeks—maybe days—they will see, they will *all* see, what beauty is, what perfection is. They will—"

"Doctor," Hund interrupted. "We're on a schedule."

"We're on *my* schedule," Roach snapped, "and don't you forget it!" He slipped the Protocol cube into a secure case. "I'm not pleased with your performance today."

"The operation was a complete success."

"In the end, yes. But you missed Dr. Solomon during the first sweep, then lost her nephew."

"He's six flights underground, with a bullet in his leg and a bomb ticking down."

"Still, I expect better of you, Commander."

Hund's eyes hardened. "If you weren't so slow giving me those upgrades . . ."

"Soon, Hund," Roach said. "Soon."

"The *full* upgrades, Doctor." For the first time that day, Hund actually smiled. "Subdural ilatfanium mesh and synaptic acceleration."

"Exactly as promised, yes." Roach looked at his watch. "Now where is that airlift? They're almost twelve seconds behind schedule, and—ah!"

He shaded his eyes as three huge helicopters, silent and black, dove from the dark sky to hover near the loading dock. Soldiers attached crates the size of 18-wheelers to dangling cables for transport.

"Did you discover anything about that audio in the processing lab?" Hund asked, watching the helicopters. "That voice calling my name?"

"It came from Dr. Solomon's private data sectors. She must've arranged some kind of automatic security for the boy before she died."

"Doesn't matter," Hund said. "In a few minutes, this is all gonna be a smoldering hole in the ground."

Roach cocked an eyebrow. "Isn't a thermonuclear device overkill?"

"Overkill is my middle name."

They boarded a helicopter, to fly away before the whole place blew—with me and my aunt still inside.

I was five feet below them, listening to every word. The blue shuttle the banner had mentioned was a supply monorail, part of an underground bullet-train system that served the Center.

I'd squeezed through a duct and crawled to the shuttle system. I'd found the blue line, then stopped, listening to the conversation overhead.

And I'd shivered at the tone in Roach's voice when he'd said, *In weeks—maybe days—they will all see what perfection is.*

If he stole the Protocol cube and the HostLink, nothing could stop him.

And guess what? He'd stolen the Protocol cube and the HostLink.

I hadn't done anything right. They were gonna get away with this, with looting the technology and bombing the Center. With hurting Auntie M.

In the gloomy duct, I closed my eyes.

She couldn't be dead. Maybe she was stunned, maybe comatose. Not dead. Not dead forever, like my mother and father, and never coming back.

You know how I said I don't remember my parents? Well, I don't—but I've seen pictures. I've seen video. I've watched my mother holding me, this squirmy pink infant, in her lap and kissing the soles of my chubby feet. I remember the look in her eyes, the expression of awe and adoration.

I'd never gotten that, the misty-eyed delight, from Auntie M. Instead, I'd gotten love; I'd gotten guidance; I'd gotten solidity. I'd gotten the ironclad guarantee that she'd always be there for me.

Always. And you know what? She'd never let me down. Not once.

And now she'd gone and left me forever, like my parents?

No, I couldn't accept that. If only I could get to her somehow, drag her away from the Center, away from the explosion . . .

Then the speakers said, "Detonation sequence in two minutes."

Two minutes until the explosion, and my aunt was at least five minutes away.

Well, you've seen it on TV a hundred times: There's a chase, and the hero's partner gets shot. He tells the hero to go on without him, but the hero never does. Instead, he grabs his buddy and brings him out alive. That's why he's the hero.

I guess I'm no hero.

The shuttle door opened. I hesitated a moment. Then I stepped inside, and the door closed behind me.

I still have nightmares about that. Leaving her behind.

Your only option was retreat, Douglas. Even if you could have dragged my body from the

Center—a physical impossibility—I was beyond your help.

Maybe.

Anyway, I got into the shuttle and looked through a window. I saw the last of the crates—the HostLink—being lifted to a helicopter.

Then things got even stranger.

DOUBLE CLICK *THIS*

I stood beside the shuttle window, scared and shaking and imagining all the terrible things I wanted to happen to Roach. I won't go into detail, but I was hitting him with some very nasty vibes.

I mean, pure *dripping* evil.

Then I felt another dizzy spell: the shuttle seemed to tilt crazily around me, and I dropped to my knees and felt something click in my head.

Hard to describe. Like when you're looking at a jigsaw puzzle and the right piece suddenly clicks in your mind. Everything comes together in a sudden deciphering and you *know* the piece fits. That's what I felt in that moment.

The cable holding the HostLink snapped.

The sheared end of the cable whipped through the air with

a shrill whistle, and the HostLink crashed to the parking lot, transforming instantly from $250 million of biodigital wizardry into $1.95 of scrap metal.

I did that. I snapped the cable.

I didn't know how, but I snapped that cable.

Your inborn ability to cause mishaps with electronic devices was magnified and focused when the Holographic Hub compromised your brain waves.

Yeah, we know that *now*, that falling into the Holographic Hub juiced my streetlight-flickering and kiln-zapping skills. And the first thing I'd snapped was that cable.

But at the time, I had no idea how I'd done that—or even if I really had.

I freaked.

Still dizzy, I barely managed to pull myself to my feet and started hammering on the shuttle door, trying to get out. I don't even know where I wanted to go: back into the bomb zone?

Not smart, even for me.

But I'd lost it. So I pushed. I pulled. Nothing.

I slumped against the wall in defeat. Then:

Shhhhhhhhhhhhhhhhhhhh.

The sound of the shuttle door unsealing. I turned, and the edges of my vision darkened into a tunnel.

The door slid open. I saw that someone was out there. Some*thing*.

I looked for a long moment.

Then everything went black.

DROPPING THE EAVES

"That's the boy?" a deep male voice said.

"Kind of scrawny," a female voice answered.

"Cut him a little slack," a different man said. "He took a bullet in the leg—oh, and saved the world."

"The world?"

"If Roach had stolen that HostLink, not even *we* could've stopped him. At least now we have a chance. The kid bought us time."

"He's still scrawny," the female said.

PLAN B

One of the things you learn when you're fighting a supergenius like Roach is that there's always a plan B. And a plan C. And D, E, and F.

And don't get me started on plans G through R.

The guy *never* ran out of plans. Ever.

I didn't know this at the time, but in Roach's helicopter, he and Hund looked at the smoke curling from the wreckage of the HostLink.

"Someone's gonna pay for that," Hund spat. "With blood."

"Most assuredly," Roach said.

"What now? We've got nothing."

Roach slipped the Protocol cube from his pocket. "Wrong, Commander. We have Plan B. Instead of a single, massive scan, we'll progress in stages."

"You mean digitize them a few at a time?"

"Precisely. We'll scan in a dozen and use them to power our scans of the next hundred. Then those hundred will prepare my servers to scan the next thousand—and the ten thousand after that."

"Won't they notice?"

Roach chuckled drily. "The idiot meatpeople, trapped in meatspace? Until I show them the glory of cyberspace, they'll always be sluggish and stupid and disconnected. They notice nothing at all."

"When do we start?"

"Immediately. Look down. See that nice little town?"

Hund nodded. "Sure."

"Tomorrow, that town will be pristine: a stream of pure ones and zeros. And after I scan them, my research will progress by great leaps. Oh, the experiments I'll perform! The freedom they'll discover from those fleshy anchors—"

</RANT>

Yeah, a little of Roach's ranting goes a long way.

The thing is, I guess I stopped him from scanning in thousands—tens of thousands, millions—of people at once. Which was good.

Go me.

But Roach seemed pretty content to take this one step at a time. To scan hundreds of people into his machine first. To run experiments on them. To make his digital realm stronger and stronger every time he digitized another brain, ended another life. To exploit the power of scanned minds as his own private data banks.

Starting with my hometown.

And I'm no hero. I know that. If you've read this whole blog, you know that, too. I'm just an ordinary kid . . . with one quirk. And some friends.

Of course, I hadn't even met them yet. Right then, I was unconscious in the blue shuttle, a hundred feet underground, hurtling away from the nuclear blast at ninety-five miles per hour.

Good thing they used a "cone" nuke, one of Roach's inventions, which funneled the blast into a small perimeter and minimized fallout. See, that way—

Douglas.

Yeah?

You are done posting for today.

What are you talking about? I can't end with me unconscious. I mean, Roach *still* got 99 percent of everything he wanted, and planned to scan in my town the next day. All my teachers, all my friends . . . Jamie.

You haven't yet started your science assignment, which is due tomorrow.

Well, the due date is kinda flexible.

I am monitoring your teacher's computer. The due date is tomorrow, with no extensions. And you are currently receiving a C in class.

A C? Sheesh. I'm aiming for a B-minus.

Still, I'm not really done with this—

You lived, Douglas. You saved the Protocol and the skunks. You smashed the HostLink.

I didn't keep that Memory Cube from Hund. I didn't save my aunt.

Without you, we'd have lost already. Take your victories as they come.

NOBODY READS MY BLOG

After all these posts, my blog traffic is still pathetic. But I don't care. I'm gonna keep writing.

Maybe one day more people will stumble across this. Maybe one day they'll understand.

For those of you who aren't only reading, but actually e-mailed . . . thanks. We're investigating every report of cyber crime, every whisper of VIRUS activity. We're doing everything we can to make sure your town doesn't end up like mine.

I GOT THE B-MINUS!

Now, where was I?

Oh, right: in the shuttle, when everything went black. Time passed. A hum surrounded me, the shuttle rocked me, then a crack of thunder split the world in two.

I mumbled in my sleep and fell back into nothingness.

When I finally woke, the first thing I noticed was the smell. Before I even opened my eyes, I knew where I was.

```
CATCH THE BLUE SHUTTLE IN SUBSECTOR
2W . . . GO TO THE ROOT CANAL . . .
```

Well, I'd caught the shuttle and somehow woken in the root canal, that dark, dingy basement I'd found when I was ten. I hadn't been there in years, but I still remembered the smell.

Mud and mildew. And apparently, I'd slept on a slab of cardboard. I sat up, leaned against the dirty concrete wall, and moaned. I ached everywhere.

For a minute, I rubbed my temples and tried to convince myself that I'd had a bad dream. That everything that had happened the night before . . . hadn't happened. The explosions, the gunshot, the look in Hund's eyes when he drew his knife.

My aunt lying motionless on the floor.

A wonderful vacation from reality, but a lie. I knew all that had happened, all that and more.

I pressed my palms into my eyes, to rub away the cobwebs. And to keep from crying as the image of my aunt flashed inside my mind. I needed to focus. I didn't even know how I'd gotten there. I stared into the dark corners of the cellar. At least I was alone.

First I needed to call the cops. My aunt was dead. If Roach's scanning her brain into his machine hadn't killed her, then the tactical nuke had.

No way around that. I needed to tell the cops.

Plus I'd seen Roach and Hund invade the Center with a mercenary force and steal millions of dollars in biodigital tech. Oh, and I'd snapped a cable with my mind—though I didn't *know* that then but only suspected.

Still, on second thought, if I told the cops *everything*, they'd send me to a psych ward. Maybe I'd just give them the abbreviated version.

So I stood and stretched and rubbed my bruises. Then I stepped toward the crumbling stairs—and froze.

A shadow fell across the stairs. Someone was coming into the root canal. Someone coming for *me*.

CATCHING THE BUG

This is what I imagined was stalking down the steps into the root canal:

I backed into the darkness and groped around until I found a nice-sized rock. I breathed through my mouth, trying to stay completely silent.

And as the shadow loomed closer, I tensed. No way was one of Hund's soldiers gonna corner me in here. I'd bust his head open first.

The shadow stepped into the room and I lunged forward, swinging the rock.

"Bug?" the shadow said.

Jamie!

I had too much momentum to stop the swing, so I heaved the rock past Jamie, barely missing her head, and lost my balance. I stumbled and knocked her to the ground, sending her laptop crashing down.

"Bug!" She cursed at me. "Right in the dirt!"

"Sorry."

"Who were you expecting, an ax murderer?"

"Worse," I said.

She grabbed her laptop, then eyed me. "You look terrible. What happened last night?"

"What *happened*? The whole place exploded—and the— the centipede saved me from that *thing*—and ohmigod, my aunt is—" I swallowed. "And Hund pulled a knife and the monkeybeast—"

"Bug!" Jamie said. "Take a deep breath."

I breathed. "Okay. Okay, everything started with the first explosion—"

"What happened to your *pants*?"

"I got shot."

She looked at my leg. "Holy crap. Are you okay?"

"Yeah. No. Kinda."

"You're starting to scare me."

"My leg's fine. Listen, these guys took over the Center and—" I stopped and stared at her. "How did you know I was here?"

"I got your e-mail," she said, checking her laptop for damage from the fall. "With all the news about an accident at the Center, I—"

"You got my *what*?"

"E-mail. To meet you here with my laptop."

My stomach twisted. "Oh, no."

"What?"

"This is bad, this is very bad. . . ."

She tapped a few keys, then looked relieved when her laptop responded. "Don't worry, it's still working. Even logs on. That's weird. You'd need a satellite to get wireless here."

"Not *that*. We're being set up, Jamie. We can't stay here."

"I'm not going anywhere until you tell me what's happening."

"Jamie," I said. "Let's go—*now*."

"First you send an e-mail saying meet you here, then—"

"I didn't send an e-mail."

"Someone spoofed your address?" She clicked her touch pad. "Who?"

"I don't know, and I don't want to find out. We have to go." I started pushing her toward the exit. "Before they show up."

"Who'd send a crazy message about blue shuttles and the root canal and—"

"The blue shuttle?" I stopped pushing. "The message mentioned the blue shuttle?"

Nobody knew about the blue shuttle except the Center's AI. And I could trust the Center's AI.

I hoped.

Then I remembered. I remembered what I'd seen outside the shuttle the night before—and I felt a little unsteady. Because what I'd seen was impossible. Some things are simply too strange to exist.

"Doug!" Jamie grabbed my arm. "Stop freaking, and tell me what's happening."

"Okay." I nodded. "Okay, where do I start?"

"At the Center last night, in your aunt's office. Something happened when you were sending me that dragonfly file for our project."

"Yeah," I said. "The building exploded. And I fell."

"Into that room, the Holographic Hub."

I nodded and looked away, afraid she'd see something different in my eyes: *brain waves compromised*. I didn't really want to think about that.

"And then," I said. "And then . . ."

A flat computer voice said, "I will provide the necessary background information."

Jamie yelped and I spun and looked frantically around the cellar. Still alone. Then, slowly, we both turned toward her laptop.

"My apologies," the laptop said. "I didn't mean to startle you."

"Jamie," I said. "That isn't funny."

"No joke," she said, looking as scared as I felt.

"Douglas," the computer said. "This is Aunt Margaret. I'm speaking to you through the laptop."

"Auntie M!" I blurted, relief washing over me. "You're alive!"

AN ERUPTION OF CORRUPTION

"Not entirely," the voice said. "I'm neither alive nor dead."

"She's alive!" I told Jamie.

"Doug, I—"

"Thank God," I breathed. "You're alive."

"Doug, shush! I'm neither alive nor dead. I'm in a liminal state. Let me tell the story."

"Fine," I said, grinning hugely. "As long as you explain words like *liminal*."

"*Liminal* means on the threshold between life and death." The laptop fell silent for a moment. "Now, Jamie, listen closely."

Jamie stared at her laptop in disbelief as my aunt told the story. The basics, at least: the mercenary attack, Roach and Hund stealing the Protocol, Roach scanning her into the Net, and me escaping in the blue shuttle.

To be honest, I didn't listen all that closely, because I was too busy doing cartwheels and setting off fireworks in my mind. I couldn't believe it. My aunt was still there, still with me. She hadn't died; she hadn't left me behind.

"What about the dragonfly?" Jamie asked when my aunt finished talking through the laptop speaker.

"Are you crazy?" I said, still smiling. "You're worried about our *homework*?"

"Not the homework! I mean on *CircuitBoard*. When you were in trouble, I saw the Holographic Hub on my computer screen. The cursor looked like a dragonfly."

"Oh," I said. "Yeah. How'd you manage to unlock the hub for me?"

"No idea." Jamie bit her lip. "I mean, I just solved the puzzles on the screen."

"Sure, you reprogrammed a military installation with a video game. And, um, what about the cable that snapped?"

"And what happened to *you*, Dr. S?" Jamie asked the laptop. "Where are you?"

"And how did I get here?" I asked. "The last thing I remember, the shuttle door opened and I saw—"

"One at a time," my aunt said through the computer. And even though it wasn't her voice, she sounded like her old self. "Jamie first. My scans reveal that the dragonfly data Doug was sending when he fell into the Holographic Hub merged with the *CircuitBoard* code on your laptop."

"Um, what?" Jamie asked.

"The Holographic Hub automatically combines, refines, and optimizes all available code," my aunt explained. "It turned your laptop into a supercomputer. The Center is gone, but your laptop is now a miniature version of the Holographic Hub. You've got more computing power than NASA."

"But . . . ," Jamie said. "How did I unlock those doors?"

"The hub also upgraded your computer game to a Net-based utility," my aunt said. "A semiautonomous codelink webform, passlocked to you alone."

"Vocabulary," I reminded her.

"Ah. Well, apparently the dragonfly probe can travel through cyberspace just like Jamie's cursor travels in the *CircuitBoard* game. Not only travel, but manipulate."

"Like a hacking tool?" I asked.

"Like an incredibly powerful hacking tool," my aunt said.

Jamie shook her head. "But what happened to *you*, Dr. Solomon? That's the most important thing. Are you . . . Where *are* you?"

"I thought you were dead," I said, my throat suddenly tight. "You were lying there . . . I thought you were dead."

"I'm sorry, Doug. I—"

"I left her there," I told Jamie. "I left her behind."

"Douglas!" my aunt said through the speaker. "I *was* dead. There was nothing you could do."

I swallowed. "I should have—"

"You were *dead*?" Jamie interrupted.

"When Roach scanned me into the Net, my body died, and he thought my mind did, too. But the Center's AI routed the data through my personal directories. Every synapse, every quark and neuron. I imprinted on the Center's intranet."

"Wait," Jamie said. "He scanned you into a machine? That's just . . . not possible."

"The technology of the Center is light-years beyond anything you can imagine."

"Okay," Jamie said, biting her lower lip. "So he scanned your brain into the Center's computers?"

"That's right. I used several sectors to protect my data, and transferred everything off-site before the final explosion."

"You mean you uploaded yourself to the Net before the bomb went off?"

"Exactly."

"So . . . where are you now?" I asked.

"Distributed through the Internet, on corporate data banks and military hardware, on home computers and telecommunications networks."

"Um. That's good, I guess."

"It is, except one of my sectors was corrupted during the transfer." There was a pause. "And the data seems to have developed a rudimentary self-consciousness."

I shook my head. "That's crazy. How do we even know you're—" I turned to Jamie. "What if this isn't my aunt?"

"I know about the root canal, Doug," the laptop said. "I know about your Spider-Man pajamas—"

"That was years ago," I said.

"And the time your Chuckle Me Aldo went on the fritz."

"Which totally wasn't my fault!"

"You flushed a stuffed animal down the toilet."

"That thing was freaky."

"The plumber cost me four hundred dollars!"

"Okay," I said to Jamie. "This is definitely Auntie M."

Jamie snorted. "Yeah, I figured." She looked at the laptop in the dim light of the dirt cellar. "What do you mean it's developing self-consciousness?"

"I don't know exactly," my aunt said. "But the corrupted sector seems to be self-aware. This new Awareness isn't just code, it's a—a person."

"Corrupted" was not precisely correct.

I'll get to that later.

ANOTHER COUNTDOWN

Jamie asked, "So after Roach scanned your mind, some of that data started . . . changing?"

"Yes. Usually before scanning in a mind, we format the computer to preserve the data exactly. But Roach wasn't trying to scan my mind; he was trying to kill me. To *erase* my mind. And it would've worked, but the Center's AI recognized me and sent the information into my personal sectors. Except nothing was formatted, so the data is behaving . . . oddly."

Jamie took a breath. "Okay. So what do we *do*? How long do you have?"

"I can maintain the integrity of my data for another three hours—"

"Three hours?" I interrupted, hope sparking in my chest. "You mean you can come back?"

"You can reconstruct your body?" Jamie asked.

"If you locate a Bio-Gen Uplink within three hours, I can rebuild my body. Otherwise, I'll remain in digital format."

"Like, forever?" Jamie asked.

"No," the laptop said. "Eventually, my data—my mind and personality—will lose coherence."

"Lose coherence?" I asked, even though I was afraid of the answer. "Vocabulary, Auntie M."

"Without access to an uplink within three hours," she said, "I won't be able to rebuild my body. I'll become pure data. And after that, my mind will die, too."

Jamie bit her lip again. "What's an uplink?"

"You mean like that HostLink thing?" I asked.

"Yes, the HostLink was effectively a superpowerful uplink. A prototype, one of a kind. Gone forever, thank God."

"Why is that a good thing?"

"Because Roach could've used it to scan in millions of people almost immediately. That's why destroying the HostLink was so important. Regular uplinks, on the other hand, just transfer digital format into biological form, and vice versa."

"Like those T-bone steaks?" I asked.

"Exactly. Except the uplinks work both ways—from digital file to physical body, and from physical body to digital file."

"The Center's a heap of charcoal," I said. "Are there any uplinks left?"

"Only three."

"Then we'll get one," I said. "Where are they?"

"Roach stole two of them last night, and the third's in a heavily guarded military installation in San Diego."

"I don't care," I said. "I left you for dead once. I'll never do that again."

And you know what?

Sure, I'm an ordinary kid, but after seeing what I'd seen the day before—after surviving what I'd survived—I didn't care. I'd get my aunt one of those uplinks if I had to crawl over broken glass.

Three hours.

I had three hours to save my aunt, to bring her back to life.

Maybe I'd never done anything with three hours before, except waste them playing video games. But this time, I would not fail.

For the first time in my life, I couldn't.

SPIN DOWN

"After I pinpoint the location of an uplink . . ." The laptop's hard drive whirred. "Your battery is damaged, Jamie. I have only thirty-eight seconds before power-down."

Jamie gave me a dirty look. "Bug knocked me over."

"Oops."

"You need to recharge the battery," Auntie M said. "And stay out of sight. They're watching for you, Doug."

"Me?" I yelped. "Who?"

"Roach and Hund. And the army. And police."

"What?"

"Roach hacked the military net—and the government, the schools, the police. He controls satellite feeds and security cameras. He edited the report from last night to show that you vandalized the Center, causing the explosion and my death."

I swore.

"On the bright side," Jamie told me, "you're famous."

"I always thought I'd be famous for my music."

"What music? You don't even play an instrument."

"Yeah, but I'm awesome at *Rock Hero Four*."

"This isn't a time for jokes," my aunt said. "They assume that you're dead, but Roach noticed the shuttle leaving. Expect him to double-check."

I opened my mouth to say something, but no words came out.

"Doug, run to Jamie's house and get online. I'll talk to you there. Keep a low profile, in case Roach is watching. Jamie, go to school and pretend none of this happened. If they realize you're absent, they'll know you're involved. And hurry."

"But—the uplinks?" Jamie said. "Three hours? We need to start—"

"Just go," my aunt said. "And be careful."

Then the laptop powered down, and we were alone.

SHOPPING TRIP

When I was a little kid, they bulldozed some fields and pastures across town and built big-box stores. Huge warehouses with acres of aisles selling everything from underwear to lawn mowers to jelly beans.

To Jamie's disgust, I liked them. I liked getting lost in there for hours, just messing around and looking at all the *stuff*. Jamie, on the other hand, headed into the city with her mom every six weeks for a whole new wardrobe.

Anyway, if you start wondering how I know what I'm about to tell you, remember what I said about digital reconstruction.

After Roach was fired from the Center, my aunt developed a technology that could eavesdrop through electronic equipment—not just security cameras and cell phones, but wireless devices and even fiber-optic outlets. And since merging with the Net, she's learned to reconstruct almost anything that happens.

And of course, breaking into personnel records is far easier.

Which is how I know that Letitia Harrod worked at Tar-Mart for eight years. She was a model employee, without a single hiccup, until early that morning, when she opened the doors and found a huge mess: security cameras ripped from the walls, packaging strewn everywhere.

They'd been robbed. So Letitia called the cops and checked the store, to figure out what had been taken. Some clothes and a bunch of equipment from the hunting and fishing section. Tools, definitely. Sporting goods. Even some toys from the children's department.

She grabbed her inventory sheet . . . then heard a noise.

The robbers were still in the store. She pressed herself against a display of nonfat cookies and trembled as she listened to them.

"Check this," one of them said. "A slingshot. You see any ball bearings?"

"Try aisle nine," came another voice, deep and slow.

"A slingshot," a female voice said disgustedly. "Grow up."

"Don't blame me," the first man said. "I'm born to not kill."

"Fine, you're stuck with nonlethal weapons . . . you don't have to *like* them so much," she said. "Is that a Ping-Pong gun?"

"You fill these balls with the right chemicals . . ."

The female snorted. "A Harley, that's what I need."

"At least you found the motorcycle chain," Deep Voice said.

"Yeah, this isn't bad," the female voice replied. "Tensile strength to eight thousand pounds. Still, I'm gonna need to special order."

"You don't have enough gear?" Deep Voice asked.

"Easy for you to say," the female said. "You *are* gear. Toss me that crowbar."

Something clanked, and Deep Voice said, "We should check on the boy, now that you're equipped."

"Our scrawny sleeping beauty," the first voice said.

"What about *her*?" the female voice asked.

Letitia shivered, like she knew they were talking about her.

"I'll fix her," the first voice said.

The owner of the first voice vaulted over four aisles of breakfast cereals and home-repair tools and landed two feet in front of Letitia.

His furry ears pricked and his muzzle rose in a smile. "Boo," he said softly.

Letitia fainted.

MY SCIENCE EXPERIMENT

We climbed the root canal stairs—a rotting wooden staircase—into the corner of the abandoned weed-ridden lot. I took a few deep breaths and blinked against the morning sun.

"I don't mind the lack of indoor plumbing," I said. "But I'd kill for a convenient tree."

"Uh," Jamie said. "Gross?"

"Well, at least I slept like a baby."

"Yeah, on soggy cardboard." She glanced at me. "You still don't remember how you got there?"

"No. I mean, I guess not."

"Which means you kinda *do* know?"

"I have a theory," I said. "The only problem is, it's insane."

"That never stopped you before."

I tried to laugh but couldn't. Why? Well, take a peek at my little Checklist of Weird:

- whispering snakeskin refrigerator
- battlefield-medic centipede
- rampaging killer monkeybeast

Fine, no problem. I hadn't collapsed into a jabbering wreck at any of that.

But those *thing*s I'd seen outside the shuttle? I couldn't handle them. Not only because the weird factor blew everything else away, but because if I saw what I *thought* I saw . . .

Then I'd created them. I'd *created* them, and that simply blew my mind.

Jamie stopped and looked at me. "Are you okay?"

"Yeah, sure. I mean, I guess." I shrugged. "I don't know."

"Oh, that's clear."

Her expression almost made me grin.

"I'm okay," I said. "I'm glad they didn't kill me."

She nodded. "I'm happy about that, too."

"And once we get Auntie M back, I'll be fine."

Jamie nodded again as we crossed the weedy lot, and we got four blocks before—

A GIRL

Okay, time out. Jamie just texted me. She wants me to describe her, I guess so you can picture us walking down the sidewalk.

She's kinda skinny. And if I remember right, she was wearing a T-shirt with this logo:

</lame>

And jeans. Probably a fancy designer brand with a goofy name. Like once she told me her jeans were "Grass Station Mars" or something.

Oh! And sneakers. Definitely sneakers.

WHERE WAS I?

Right. Jamie nodded and we—

A GIRL, CONTINUED

She texted me again. She says that describing her T-shirt isn't enough.

Fine. She's sorta tallish. Brown eyes, brown skin. Two ears, two legs. The regular number of teeth, I guess.

To be honest, I never counted them.

What I'm trying to say is we got four blocks before the cops spotted us.

Municipal Police Department
Automated Crime Report
TDS Number: 75639   Complaint Number: 200346

INCIDENT TYPE

Negligent Homicide - Criminal Trespass - Malicious Endangerment
Vandalism - Destruction of Government Property

<DOMESTIC TERROR ALERT>

How Received: Radio
Car Number: 04/K
District: 3
Weapon Used: Unknown (military grade)

Time of Call: 0149 HRS
Arrival Time: 0704 HRS
Copies To: Muni Court
GEO Code: 42-Y8

KNOWN SUSPECT

Name: Solomon, Douglas J.
Race: Caucasian
Home Address: 81 Park Terrace

Sex: Male
SSN: 123-12-1231
Occupation: Student

At 0704 hours, pursuant to a BOLO (Be On the Look Out), after the alleged domestic terrorist incident at the Center for Medical Innovation, Car Number 04/K identified the suspect, DOUGLAS J. SOLOMON, crossing from the north side of Elm Street at the intersection with Third Street. Accompanied by an unidentified female between the ages of 12 and 14, the suspect fled on foot, with officers in pursuit.

"I'll call my parents," Jamie said, stepping onto the sidewalk.

"What for?"

"They're *lawyers*."

"What are they gonna do, sue Roach? Or turn me in?"

"They won't turn you in."

"Yeah, the cops say I'm guilty, but they'll believe I was framed by mercenaries with monkeybeasts."

"Mm." She wrinkled her nose. "Maybe I'll call them *after* we find proof."

We stopped at the corner and I said, "Gimme your laptop."

"No way."

"You're going that way." I pointed toward school. "And I'm going to your house."

"I'm coming with you."

"Auntie M said—"

"I don't care," Jamie interrupted. "If she's in trouble, I'm gonna help."

"You want to help? Then go to school. Maybe she—"

"No way, Doug. Three hours. That's all we have."

"These people are scary," I told her. "Seriously scary."

"You're not the only one who loves her."

From her tone of voice, I knew that Jamie had made up

her mind. After a certain point, I don't argue with her. Doesn't do any good.

Still, I felt kinda odd. Usually Jamie is the good kid, the responsible one. If she started slacking, did that mean I'd need to buckle down?

Nah.

Anyway, we headed behind the Wilkersons' house—there's a shortcut through the hedge—and past the spot where we once built the Headless Snowman, and through the playground for toddlers learning to climb stairs and high schoolers learning to smoke cigarettes.

Back on the sidewalk, we turned left, and a siren SHRI*EKED*.

A police car squealed around the corner, coming fast.

I started to run toward Jamie's house, but Jamie yelled, "This way!" and took off toward the school.

I followed close behind.

We cut through the Nguyens' backyard, around the swimming pool, where ~~Stacy Nguyen sunbathed~~ a cop car couldn't follow. We ran behind the garden shed and into Mrs. Klein's yard, then alongside the Coopers' porch.

This was our neighborhood, and we knew every inch, better than anyone: they weren't gonna catch us here.

"Where are we going?" I asked.

"To school."

"You just said you *weren't* going to school."

"You'll be harder to spot there; we'll blend."

"That's your plan? We'll blend?"

"Well, Doug"—she grinned over her shoulder—"nobody's better than you at disappearing into a crowd at school."

I snorted. "True enough."

My dad had been a professor, and my mom an engineer, so I guess the teachers had pretty high expectations of me—at least, at first. That was probably why I'd developed my ability to avoid attention, learning how to hide in plain sight to keep them from calling on me all the time. And the truth is . . . Well, Auntie M said I wasn't afraid of attention; I just didn't like people wanting me to live up to their memory of my parents. Like I was afraid I'd disappoint them or something.

I dunno, maybe she was right. Still, knowing how to disappear into a crowd was a good skill to have right then.

We slipped behind the mini-mart, then hopped the fence onto the school's upper field.

"First stop, the computer lab," Jamie said. "We'll get in touch with your aunt. Ask her what to do next."

"If we're separated, let's meet at . . ." I thought for a second while we cut across the baseball diamond. "The drainage pipe in that ditch across the street."

Jamie shuddered. "What's with you and repulsive pits today?"

"It's the perfect place. Nobody'll look there."

"Fine," she said. "*Outside* the drainage pipe."

"Sure, that's what I meant."

When we got to the pitcher's mound, Jamie cocked her head. "What's that?"

"What?" Then I heard it: *whapwhapwhapwhap*. "Oh."

"Look." Jamie pointed into the sky, at a distant tiny speck, no larger than the period at the end of this sentence.

Except getting bigger. . . . • • ● ● ● ●

Fast.

And louder: *WHAPWHAPWHAPWHAPWHAPWHAPWHAP*.

A helicopter.

No. A helicopter *gunship*. Swooping directly at us.

Jamie gasped. "Ohmigod."

"Um," I said. *"Run!"*

I grabbed her hand and yanked her toward school. We needed to get off the field, we needed cover—we needed something between us and that gunship.

But when we turned, guess what we saw?

Another helicopter, swooping down. We were trapped in the middle, sitting ducks between two, um, things that hunted ducks.

Well, long story short: the helicopters landed at each end of the field, trapping us between.

"Great," I said. "We'll blend."

SURRENDER

Soldiers poured from the helicopters, fanning into semicircles and pointing assault rifles at us.

"Lie facedown," one of the soldiers bellowed. "Hands behind your head."

I looked at Jamie. She looked at me.

We both looked at the soldiers.

Then we lay down and put our hands behind our heads.

AT LEAST THEY'RE NOT LITTLE YAPPY DOGS

We were surrounded. The soldiers prowled forward, rifles raised.

"They're just kids," one soldier muttered.

"That kid detonated a nuke at the research site," said another. "If they move, you are cleared to fire."

"I didn't detona—" I started.

"No talking!" a soldier yelled.

"He didn't do anything," Jamie said.

"If they *talk*, you're cleared to fire," the same guy said.

Then one of them knelt on my back. Which hurt pretty bad. He yanked at my arms and handcuffed me.

"Oww," Jamie said, lying next to me.

"Suspects secure, Captain," one of the soldiers said. "And ready for transport."

A huge crash sounded at the far end of the field.

I scrunched around to see what had happened, and for a second couldn't understand what I was looking at. Lying on my stomach handcuffed, I didn't have the best vantage point. Then I realized that one of the helicopters was upside-down.

And burning.

And . . . crumpled.

Around me, the soldiers reacted. Some of them shouted orders, and others fell to the ground, taking aim. Because in front of the burning helicopter, three . . . *figures* stepped from a cloud of black smoke.

For a second, I thought they were wearing gorilla suits. But those weren't suits. And they weren't gorillas.

"Are those . . . skunks?" Jamie murmured.

Yeah, they were skunks. I'd seen them before, outside the blue shuttle the previous night.

Skunk-people. Your basic skunk-people.

And you know what? I could accept a talking snake fridge and a centipedal medic. They'd done crazy cutting-edge stuff at the Center, patching together technology and biology. Heck, I'd even learned to live with a monkeybeast.

But *skunks*?

Yeah, skunks. With short black fur and white stripes that

rose to Mohawks atop their heads. Big bushy black-and-white tails and kinda skunky-looking faces. And humanoid, human-size bodies, heavy on the weight lifting.

Well, mostly humanoid. The big one—Larkspur—looked a little android, too, given he was mostly encased in BattleArmor.

The female—Poppy—wore a leather jacket and biker boots and swung a chain in one hand and wielded a crowbar in the other. She'd been output through the *Street Gang* video game while it was running the Hog Stompers versus the Fists of Kung Fu.

And the last one—Cosmo—looked like a fuzzy Punisher, in combat gear with a bandoleer full of gadgets I didn't recognize. He'd emerged from the VR combat simulator, with knowledge of a million combat scenarios.

One squad of soldiers advanced warily, yelling at the skunks to raise their hands and lie facedown and drop their weapons—all at once.

"I am Larkspur," Larkspur told the soldiers, his voice a deep rumble. The morning sun glinted off his armor-encased body. But he wasn't just *wearing* the Quantuum 19 BattleArmor prototype, he *was* the Quantuum 19 BattleArmor. "The boys come with us."

"Boys!" Jamie hissed under her breath.

Great. I was shaking with fear, and Jamie was insulted that a skunk—a skunk!—thought she was a boy.

"Smooth move, big guy," said Cosmo, twirling a handful of darts. Why darts? Because some bored technician had loaded his favorite game—*SimToys*—into the VR combat simulator. "That one's a girl."

"Pardon me," Larkspur said to Jamie.

Poppy didn't say anything. She just stood there, smiling at the soldiers and lazily swinging her motorcycle chain, her eyes eager and alert.

"Throw down your weapons," a soldier said.

"That is not possible," Larkspur told him.

"Down! Now! *Down!*" the soldiers yelled.

"I'm afraid we cannot comply with your request," Larkspur said. "We are—"

"Open fire!"

I must've blinked, because Poppy had been standing thirty feet from the soldiers—then she was among them. Her chain lashed the rifles from two soldiers' hands, and she dropped low and swept two other guys from their feet with a flashing kick, then leapt and spun, all in one movement, tossing a soldier halfway across the field.

The soldiers started firing.

Jamie and I hugged the ground.

And Larkspur moved.

He's big and talks slow and steady, so you might think he can't move that fast. And maybe he's not as quick as

Poppy—when she gets going, she's just a blur—but Larkspur is faster than anything human. Not even close.

The soldiers fired, and I don't know if they hit him. Doesn't really matter. Regular bullets bounce right off him. He knocked a few heads, pausing only to bend a rifle into a U with his bare hands.

Show-off.

And Cosmo? He stood in back and threw the darts. Not *at* the soldiers, though; he tossed them away from all the fighting, in the opposite direction. I had no idea why.

Still, a minute later the skunks were the only ones left standing. The soldiers lay in moaning heaps around the field.

"Time to leave," Larkspur said. "Reinforcements incoming, with heavy armaments."

"Good," Poppy said with a predatory grin. "I need the workout."

"We have a deadline." Larkspur checked one of the dials on his wrist monitor. "And we don't want to hurt anyone."

"Speak for yourself."

"Cosmo," he said. "Remove the handcuffs."

"Who died and made you king, Tin Man?" Cosmo said. But he came over and snapped our cuffs.

As I write this now, the skunks look normal to me—well, *almost* normal—but at the time, they blew my mind. Walking, talking skunk-people.

"Y-You were there last night," I stammered. "At the Center. Outside the shuttle."

"Saved your little pink butt," Poppy told me.

"He saved ours, as well," Larkspur said.

"My butt," Poppy said, "is not pink."

"Are we standing here talking about butts?" Cosmo asked. "Because I'm pretty sure we're standing here talking about butts."

Poppy looked at Jamie. "Who's the girl?"

"I'm Jamie," she said. "Who are—what are—who—"

"What is this? Interspecies social hour?" Cosmo said.

"I see you've secured the laptop," Larkspur told Jamie. "Good. Back to the root canal."

"Um," Jamie said, staring at his looming armor-and-fur form.

"Yes?"

"Um," Jamie said, still staring.

He knelt beside her, his deep voice a gentle rumble. "We should go, before they return."

"The battery's dead," Jamie told him. "We were heading to my house to recharge."

He cocked his huge head. "Then shall we join you?"

Jamie and I looked at each other, unable to believe we were chatting with a bunch of life-size, combat-ready, steroid-abusing Muppets.

"Dr. Solomon stressed the need for urgency," Larkspur murmured.

"You know my aunt?" I asked.

"Yes," he said. "And her time is running out."

That got through to me. I said I'd crawl over broken glass to help my aunt: skunk-people were nothing.

"Yeah," I said. "Join us."

After a moment, Jamie nodded and said, "This way," and led the skunks toward her house.

We walked past the darts Cosmo had thrown to the side of the field. They were stuck in the ground in this shape:

$$; -)$$

That was what he'd been doing: making a dart smiley.

SUBURBAN RECON

When we left the school grounds, Larkspur stayed with us while Cosmo disappeared into the shadow of one house and Poppy bounded onto the roof of another.

"Police patrols," Larkspur explained. "They'll divert them, then meet us at Jamie's house."

"Divert them how?" Jamie asked. "I mean . . ."

"Various methods. None of which, I hope, will flatten the entire neighborhood."

She looked at him like she couldn't tell if he was kidding. "Oh."

"They are sometimes a little too . . . enthusiastic," he said.

"Yeah, I'm getting that." Then she said, "Digitized skunks?"

"Indeed."

"Generated through damaged output paths?" she asked. "BattleArmor and combat sims and biker ninjas?"

Larkspur nodded his armored head. "And 9,692,000 iterations."

"What does that mean?" she asked.

"You know there are 525,600 minutes in a year?"

Jamie nodded. "Everyone knows that, but—"

"Everyone does *not* know that," I interrupted.

"But who cares?" she continued.

"Imagine that each iteration is one minute," Larkspur said. "Nine million, six hundred and ninety-two thousand iterations."

"You mean you . . . you lived through all those iterations?" Jamie asked, her eyes glittering with excitement. "You *experienced* them? Inside the Center's data banks?"

He nodded. "We learned. We evolved. We were born yesterday, but—"

"You're eighteen." She turned to me with the same

expression she gets when she finishes a science experiment. "They're eighteen years old."

"So they can drive and vote," I said. *"After we save my aunt."*

We walked the rest of the way to her house in silence.

A CASE OF VIRAL INFECTION

"I've died and gone to girly heaven," Poppy said sarcastically, prowling into Jamie's bedroom.

Jamie's room isn't actually that girly. More a weird mixture of pink frilly things from when she was a kid, expensive furniture and designer clothes, and science-geek stuff.

"The garage is downstairs," Jamie replied. "If you want to pour a can of engine oil over your head."

Poppy gave Jamie a dirty look and tossed five of her stuffed animals into the air. She spun and flipped and kicked them all around the room, and one bounced off Larkspur's shoulder, but he didn't notice. He was too busy at Jamie's laptop, logging on to the Net. Meanwhile, Cosmo was in the corner, fiddling with a few toys he'd grabbed at the big-box store, a heap of circuits he'd ripped from the camcorder downstairs, and some cleaning products from under the kitchen sink.

And I was sitting there staring. I still couldn't believe it. Skunk-people.

"I'm on," Larkspur said.

In a moment, my aunt's voice came over Jamie's speakers. "Poppy!" she said. "Stop that and pay attention. You too, Cosmo."

To my surprise, Poppy and Cosmo listened to her and gathered around the computer.

"This is the situation. We have approximately two hours to get an uplink. If we fail, I'll die—and the skunks will revert to pure information."

"Pure information?" Larkspur asked.

Poppy grunted. "Sounds nasty."

"Your new state is highly volatile," my aunt explained. "If you don't stabilize with an uplink, say good-bye to your opposable thumbs. You'll dissolve into a bundle of digital information."

"I *like* my thumbs," Cosmo said.

"You've located the uplinks?" Larkspur asked my aunt.

"There are three," she said. "Roach has two and the third is in a military installation in San Diego."

"Give us Roach's address." Cosmo cracked his knuckles. "I'd like to break down his front door."

"And both his legs," Poppy added.

"Roach's encryption is too strong," my aunt said. "I'm still working on locating him."

Larkspur nodded. "San Diego, then."

"We don't have time to go all that way," Jamie said.

"Yeah," I said. "And unless the uplink's at the San Diego Zoo, aren't the skunks gonna attract a little attention, driving down the road?"

"For the skunks," my aunt said, "the 'information super-highway' really is a highway. They can travel thousands of miles in a second. If there's a sufficient concentration of technology at their destination, they'll be able to reanimate inside the military installation."

"Out of *nothing*?" Jamie asked.

"Of course not," my aunt said. "You know better than that. Think it through."

Jamie bit her lip. "They'll reanimate from . . . from whatever atoms are in the area? The background radiation from any electronics will reshape the particles into their forms!"

"Very good," my aunt said. "They're the only digital life-forms that don't need an uplink or those 'steaks' Doug used. At least, once they get stabilized. They'll jack into the Net here, reanimate in San Diego to grab the uplink, and—"

"Hold on," I said. "Wait one second."

"Yes?"

"First, there are talking skunks in the room."

"Yes, Doug, I'm aware that you in particular have seen some odd things—"

"This whole thing is insane. The Muppets here—"

Poppy growled at me.

"No offense," I quickly added. "The skunks are gonna zap across the country in streams of . . . of . . . of—"

"Electrons?" Jamie guessed.

"Muons and hadrons—" my aunt started.

"In streams of *whatever*," I said. "They'll break into a military installation and steal an uplink? Yes? Good. They'll reanimate you. Which is great, that's the entire point—"

"Also," Cosmo muttered, "I want to keep my thumbs."

"Yeah, and the skunks get stabilized. I guess that's good, too. But then what? The whole U.S. government is after me. Roach and Hund are still out there and—"

"VIRUS," my aunt said.

"Huh?"

"They call themselves VIRUS."

"At least they're honest," Jamie said.

"Not at all," my aunt said. "They're posing as a political movement. VIRUS. The Virtual Republic for Upgrading Society."

"Virus," Jamie said. "Cute."

"They're getting some press, too. They claim they'll end poverty and war, hunger and sickness—all the problems in the world—by scanning people into the Net."

"All the problems," Poppy said. "Like freedom, independence—"

"Humor," Cosmo added. "Creativity—"

"Roach plans," my aunt interrupted, "to digitize everything, to reproduce reality as virtual reality. Then he'll destroy the real world—with nukes or biological weapons—leaving him programmer king of the digital world he's created, running on automated servers in underground bunkers."

"And he'll have his trigger finger on the Delete key," Larkspur said.

"Exactly."

"No way," I said. "That's just . . . No way."

"Bug," Jamie said. "You're arguing with your aunt . . . who's *inside a computer*."

"Jamie's right, Doug. My body died last night. I'm already a virtual life-form."

"Fine," I said. "We need the uplink. Then what?"

"Roach must have a central data bank," Larkspur said, thinking out loud. "Something like a . . . a virtual city he uses as a base."

"That's right," my aunt said. "Without the HostLink, he'll need to start smaller, to build his domain from a central location. Digitize a few minds at a time—and bodies, too, if he's using his scanning booths. First a handful of victims, then a hundred. Then thousands and millions . . ."

When my aunt's voice trailed off, Larkspur nodded. "How long until he starts?"

"I'm not sure," my aunt said from inside the computer.

"But I aim to find out. While you're getting the uplink, we'll be doing some research."

"We?" Jamie said. I could tell she liked the sound of that.

"Fasten your dragonfly," my aunt said. "We're going for a ride."

THE FERRARI'S IN THE SHOP

A few minutes later, I showed the skunks to the three-car garage. I opened the door and Poppy snarled when she saw the only car there: Jamie's parents' minivan.

"No way," Poppy said. "I am not riding in *that*."

"It's only a half mile to the electric company substation where we can jack in," Larkspur said. "At least you fit."

He had a point. If he didn't curl on his side in the back, his head would pop through the roof.

"I need a Harley," she said. "Okay? I *need* a Harley."

"I'm thinking a skateboard," Cosmo said.

"That nonlethal setting is one thing," she grumbled, "but what is *with* you?"

"A few too many iterations in *SimToys*," Larkspur said.

"Or roller skates," Cosmo continued.

"Roller—" Poppy spun around. "Okay, Cosmo. Right here. Let's go."

"Which one of you wants to drive?" Larkspur asked as he squeezed into the back.

Poppy and Cosmo looked at each other; then they looked at me.

"Throw the keys between us, Bug," Poppy said.

I saw where this was going. I tossed the keys and leapt backward.

Poppy and Cosmo moved lightning fast. She launched forward and he pivoted, and I heard the smack of blows falling without actually seeing the punches. Then she swept Cosmo's ankles from under him and he twisted her arm while backflipping.

After another flurry of blows, she somersaulted over him and landed in a combat crouch. With the keys in her hand.

She dangled them at Cosmo, teasing him. But you can't out-tease Cosmo: during the fight, he'd slipped a pair of little devil horns—Jamie's Halloween costume from the year before—onto Poppy's head.

"Nice horns," he said.

She cocked her head, confused. Then she felt them. She reached up, took the horns off, and stepped toward him threateningly. He backed off and raised his hands.

"Fine," he said. "You drive. You'll look great sitting behind the wheel of this beautiful luxury automobile."

He patted the dusty minivan.

After they drove off, I went back to Jamie's bedroom and watched her fool around with *CircuitBoard* on her laptop. The screen looked a little like . . . a circuit board. Except more colorful and animated.

"Where's the Fire button?" I asked, sitting beside her.

"Bug." Jamie snorted. "You know there's no Fire button."

"Then how're you supposed to shoot?"

"You're not. You have to use your brain instead."

"Well, that's no fun," I said. "Auntie M, you there?"

"Right here," the laptop said.

"What's our job, then?"

"To locate Roach," my aunt said. "To find any trace of him."

"What, you mean search for him online?" I asked.

"Not exactly. Larkspur synced Jamie's laptop with the Protocol, and I'm finishing a little . . . custom coding right now. There."

"All done?" Jamie asked.

"Give her a test-drive," my aunt said.

Jamie pressed Go on the *CircuitBoard* menu and the dragonfly appeared on-screen.

"Looking good," my aunt's voice said. "Let me connect you to one of the central Reslocs."

The screen fuzzed for a second, then refocused. We were

online. And let me try to express, in one word, what we saw: the most boring spreadsheet in the world.

That is seven words, Douglas.

Don't blame me. I was too bored to count.

We saw code directories and text flows and line after line of numbers. Looked like a math textbook from hell.

"I'll direct you toward Roach's point of origin," my aunt said. "I suspect he's routed through Resloc 87u23bi94-13."

"Why don't *you* search?" I asked.

"I'm overextended. I'm trying to deal with this new Awareness—"

"The corrupt data?"

"The corrupt data from my *brain*," she said. "It seems to be trying to communicate with me. Besides, the dragonfly is a perfect observation and research tool."

"Yeah, but it can't actually *do* anything," I said. "Like shoot."

"You don't need to shoot, Doug. You need to gather information. Good luck."

"Wait!" I said. "How much time do you have?"

"Less than two hours."

Then she was gone.

Jamie connected the joystick I'd given her a few months earlier in a failed attempt to teach her to play *Arsenal Five*, and in a second, the dragonfly started moving.

Jamie isn't much for real video games, but I have to admit she was good at this. She followed the information flows toward the Resloc (which is some kind of Net address I don't understand) my aunt had mentioned. She wormed her way in somehow—matching packets, she said—and we were there.

Everything changed.

From text screens and spreadsheet columns to streaming graphics, like an animated film. Incredible, with crisp glowing rivers of data and bulbous memory buffers and flowing software shapes.

Amazing. And this was only the outskirt of Roach's domain.

Jamie buzzed around for a few minutes, getting the hang of the controls in the new environment.

"You want me to try?" I asked.

"The dragonfly's coded to me," she said. "Besides, you'd probably start chasing after a carapace gun."

"Carapace *rifle*." I watched her for another minute. "Actually, you're good with that thing."

A little smile curved at her mouth. "Thanks."

"Weird, because you're crap at *HARP*."

"*HARP* is a lame—ooh, what's that?" She darted the dragonfly toward a scrolling spiral of information. "That's the Resloc. Now we start downloading."

She buzzed through thousands of gigabytes of memory stacks, darting through directories and file structures, drilling deeper and deeper into the information, chasing that Resloc . . . until she emerged on the other side.

We gasped.

"That's—" she said, then stopped, staring as streaming video replaced the data files.

"The auditorium," I finished. "At school."

On her screen, we saw two things:

Our school auditorium. The real place, in real time, the dragonfly somehow tapping into a video feed.

A virtual auditorium, faint and cartoonish, superimposed behind the real one like a shadow.

And inside the real auditorium?

Fear. Tears and whimpers. Dread.

Right now—watching live—we saw our entire neighborhood crammed inside the auditorium. Our neighbors and teachers and friends packed, sardine-tight, in a cramped line that snaked across the floor and disappeared through the double doors.

Little kids wept. Couples held hands tight. Everyone looked scared—the teachers, the firefighters. The people in business suits, the kids in fast-food uniforms. Letitia Harrod, the woman who worked at Tar-Mart.

Worse than scared. *Terrified.*

At each of the exits stood two heavily armed VIRUS soldiers, and a dozen more patrolled the line.

Keeping people quiet.

Keeping them frightened.

And Roach stood, with Hund by his side, at a glossy black booth on the stage. One of his scanning booths.

"Next!" Roach said.

The soldiers shoved the person in front—Mrs. Calloway, the school nurse—into the booth. The door shimmered closed and Roach pressed a button.

Nothing much happened in the auditorium, but back in Jamie's bedroom?

The lights dimmed briefly, like that scanning booth sucked all the electricity from the town's grid. Then the door shimmered open and Mrs. Calloway was gone.

Just . . . gone.

"She must've—" Jamie spoke in a horrified whisper. "They must've pulled her out the other side."

"Except they didn't," I said. "What's that?" I touched the monitor, where a row of faint oblong icons appeared.

Jamie buzzed the dragonfly over and tapped a few *CircuitBoard* commands. And when the next person—our mailman—was pushed into the machine, another oblong object appeared.

"That's a biodigital data file," Jamie gasped. "He's already started."

"You mean . . . *that's* Mrs. Calloway?"

"What's left of her."

"He's scanning our entire neighborhood."

"Not just their minds—their bodies, too. That's why he's using that booth."

"This is what my aunt meant about him starting small?"

"Yeah, the people he scans today will slave away for him in cyberspace, building capacity for more and more workers until—" She suddenly looked sick. "Oh my God. Over there."

On the screen, two people stood trembling near the end of the line, holding each other tight.

"My parents," Jamie whispered.

YOU DON'T KNOW JACK

The minivan pulled to a stop in front of the electric company substation.

I'd lived five minutes away my whole life and never noticed the place: a two-story square brick building behind a chain-link fence, like a miniature power station. Exactly the sort of bland utility building you walk past every day and never see.

The skunks filed onto the sidewalk, Cosmo from behind the wheel, because Poppy just couldn't see herself driving a minivan.

"There." Larkspur pointed to an array of satellite dishes on the substation roof. "A flux-phase transformer."

"What's a flux-phase transformer?" Cosmo asked.

"A doorway," Larkspur said. "We'll jack in there."

"Jack in?" Cosmo asked, one eyebrow twitching.

"Yes," Larkspur said. "Jack in to the Net, to travel to San Diego."

"I know what you *mean*," Cosmo said. "It just sounds funny when you say it."

"Would you prefer 'engage the biodigital transfer Protocol'?"

Poppy snorted. "Ignore him, big guy." She bounded from the street to the top of the minivan, and from there to the roof of the substation and said, "Jack in!"

"See?" Cosmo told Larkspur. "*That* is how you say it."

"Jack in!" Larkspur said in a monotone, then looked dubiously at Cosmo. "No?"

"Needs a little work," Cosmo said, and commando-climbed the wall.

Larkspur jumped. With the power of his armored legs, he can leap three or four stories straight up without trouble.

Of course, *landing* is a different story. The concrete cracked under his feet when he hit the roof near a satellite dish. "Oops."

"Which one's the trans-plotz inducer?" Poppy asked.

"The flux-phrase transformer." Larkspur pointed. "There."

It was just a metal housing, didn't look like much. But Larkspur put his hands out and stood there for a second. Then he shimmered. Flickered.

And was gone.

A moment later, Poppy followed.

Cosmo looked around. "Was it something I said?" Then he disappeared, too.

HOW ABOUT A CALCULATOR AND A FLASHLIGHT?

There's a small gray building—a shed, really—on a naval base in San Diego with a sign outside that says **LANDSCAPING**. The most boring, unimportant building around.

And you know what's inside?

Landscaping tools. Rakes, blowers, tarps.

The most boring, unimportant stuff around.

But if you look closely at the top left corner of the shed— focusing behind the cobwebs—a hidden camera scans your retinas. And if you curl your palm around the correct shovel handle, your handprint and heartbeat signature are measured and identified. And if you hold still for four seconds, you're inspected inside and out—with X-ray, CAT scan, and feature recognition.

Then, if you pass all those tests, plus a voiceprint match

during which you say the correct password, the shed works like an elevator, dropping you fifteen stories underground.

Where the guards inspect you.

In other words, forget about the front door.

Which is why the skunks chose another entrance. One hundred and seventy feet below the landscaping shed, they whirred through transoptic cables, seeking output.

They couldn't reanimate just anywhere. They needed digital devices of sufficient technological complexity. I'm not sure exactly what that means, but—

The data that composes the skunks' "real world" forms requires a three-phase biogenic mapping conduit, which can be approximated through the radiant quantum excitation of—

Enough, enough!

All she's saying is they can't transform from digital information to superskunks with just an electric toothbrush and a lightbulb; they need heavy-duty technology.

Anyway, they were searching for output and found a bank of Cray workstations—out-of-date but powerful—running low-priority applications in a dark and empty room.

Perfect.

"Did anyone catch the football scores on the way through the Net?" Cosmo asked as he flickered into solidity.

Larkspur ignored him and checked his wrist display.

"The uplink's down the hall. Room C-11." He opened the door. "Shall we?"

BABIES DON'T SHOOT BACK

Fifteen seconds later, the door to room C-11 smashed open.

Four technicians were inside, wearing white lab coats and sneakers. For a moment, they stared blankly at the broken door, like they couldn't comprehend what had happened. Then they got a closer look at Poppy—and screamed and huddled in the corner.

"You need to work on your people skills," Cosmo said, entering behind her.

Poppy ignored him and they fanned out, searched the room, and found the uplink, which looked like a cross between a fire hydrant and a high-tech bubble gum machine. Easy as that. Except in the corner, one of the technicians slowly moved her hand toward an alarm switch. None of the skunks noticed.

"Easy as stealing hair from a wig shop," Cosmo said.

Poppy looked at him. "What are you talking about?"

"It's like 'easy as taking candy from a baby.'"

"Then just say, 'easy as taking candy from a baby.'"

"That's just *mean*," Cosmo said. "Taking candy from babies."

"Larkspur?" Poppy said. "Would you tell him?"

Larkspur tucked the uplink under his arm, and the technician in the corner flicked the switch.

A siren shrieked.

The skunks looked at one another.

Poppy smiled. "This may not be a waste of time after all," she said.

She pulled her crowbar and bounded into the hall.

WITH HIS TEETH

"My parents," Jamie whispered.

We watched them on the screen. Moving closer. Closer to being absorbed into the machine.

"We have to call the cops," I said.

"The cops are after you."

"We'll leave an anonymous tip."

"Look closer, Bug." She tapped the monitor. "Right there."

The town cops. Standing in line with everyone else. Their guns had been taken away and they looked as scared as the rest of the people.

"How about the . . . the National Guard?" I asked.

"There's no time. That line gets shorter every minute."

"Can you—" I tried to think. "Can you shut them down with *CircuitBoard*?"

She nodded, her lips thin. "Let's see."

On the screen the dragonfly zipped around furiously, and her fingers blurred on the keyboard. I didn't say anything—hardly even breathed—just sat quietly, fingers crossed.

Then she said, "No. His security is too good."

"Well, um . . . ," I said.

"Maybe if we create a diversion," she said.

"This isn't TV, Jamie. This is real life."

"My parents are in there," she said. "We'll sneak into the basement and turn off the power. Then, in the confusion—"

"Forget it," I snapped. "I'm not getting within a mile of Hund."

"Doug," Jamie said.

"He's a walking nightmare. There's nothing we can do."

"My parents are in there."

"Hund'll catch us," I said. "And tear out our throats."

"Then I'll go alone," she said.

OUR ROBOT OVERLORDS

By the time Cosmo and Larkspur joined Poppy in the hallway, she was tossing the third security guard into a heap.

Larkspur eyed the moaning pile of guards. "Be gentle with the humans."

"I didn't break anything," she said. "Well, nothing *important*."

He snorted. "We have the uplink. Let's go."

"C'mon," Poppy said. "I'm just getting warmed up."

Then a mechanized voice came over the public-address system: "Code seven intrusion. Clear corridors. Guards return to stations."

"Listen to that," Poppy said. "You knock down three and the rest give up. Pathetic."

The skunks turned toward the Cray room, and—

CHUNG. CHUNG. CHUNG.

Cosmo pricked his ears. "We have company."

"I hope they wanna play rough," Poppy said, swinging her chain.

"There's no time," Larkspur said. "Back to the Cray room. We need to jack in."

Cosmo led the way. Poppy hesitated for a moment, but Larkspur's huge metal hand spun her around, and she followed.

"This time," Cosmo said, turning the corner in front of them, "someone check the football scores. The Titans are playing the . . . urk!"

"The *Urk*?" Poppy said. "What are you—"

She stopped when Cosmo's body flew past her.

And from around the corner rolled a security droid, an

armored robot with a segmented cylindrical body swaying on top of massive bulldozer treads, like a cobra rising from a basket.

Three of the droid's segments were armed. From top to bottom:

explosive mini-missiles

robotic grappling arms

short-range electrical pulses

As Poppy dove to the side, the droid hit her with enough electricity to power a small city.

She flew backward and smashed into the wall.

Then the droid fired a surface-to-surface missile at Larkspur. He dodged—I told you he was fast—but couldn't fight back, not with the uplink in his arms. He curled into a ball instead, cradling the uplink, waiting for the mini-missile to explode behind him.

Instead, it sped back the other way—screaming toward the droid.

"Right back at you," Cosmo said from behind Larkspur.

He'd caught the mini-missile in his slingshot and whipped it back—which is about as easy as catching a bullet between your teeth.

The missile hit the droid dead center. It staggered

backward, almost fell, then straightened and made a horrible shrieking noise.

"Watch your language," Cosmo said. "There are ladies present."

He glanced at Poppy, who was still slumped against the wall, and bared his fangs in a smile, which only widened when the droid sped past her, calculating that she was no longer a threat.

Here's a little hint for all you droids out there: Poppy is *always* a threat.

The droid caromed toward Cosmo, one robot arm slashing forward for a killing punch.

Which never landed.

Poppy's chain whipped around the security droid's top segment and spun it toward her. Then, using the momentum of the spin, she landed a double kick directly on its face-plate.

The droid swayed—you could tell she'd crunched some wiring inside—and shot another pulse of electricity at her.

Not fast enough, though. The bolt just singed her tail fur and blasted past.

Poppy swore and twitched her tail.

"Watch your language," Cosmo said. "There are gentle-men present."

In one smooth motion, he dove away from a mini-missile

and pulled a grenade from his belt. He hurled the grenade at the droid's robotic eyes and rolled back to his feet.

Except that was no regular grenade. That was a little device of Cosmo's own invention, combining a toy from the big-box store, some cleaning supplies, and a few circuits from Jamie's TiVo.

The "grenade" splattered over the droid's visual sensors and oozed goo: a sticky, acidic goo that corroded inorganic material. The droid shrieked again and staggered toward Poppy.

She grabbed one robot arm and levered the droid over her shoulder. It flew down the corridor, smashed through a set of double doors, and lay still.

Smoking.

"Now that," Poppy said, brushing the singed fur from her tail, "was almost a real fight."

"The uplink," Larkspur reminded them. "Dr. Solomon doesn't have much time."

They ran down the hallway toward the Cray room. Turned the corner.

And stopped.

Three more security droids were waiting for them.

SOME DAYS YOU NEED TO VENT

Maybe you've had tough-guy daydreams about charging into a desperate situation and saving the day. I know I have. But there are three things those daydreams never cover.

1. Riding your bicycle to the rescue. Not very tough-guy. You don't see Batman wearing a bike helmet. You don't see Wolverine on a Huffy.
2. Trembling from fright so hard that you can hardly stay *on* the bike.
3. Watching your plan fall apart before any of the "saving the day" stuff happens.

Of course, there was some good news, too: Jamie finally checked out the drainage pipe with me.

The drainage pipe ran from a ditch across the street into the school basement—or at least, *toward* the basement. School lore said that a bunch of kids once broke into the school through the pipe, but I'd never been able to convince Jamie to crawl inside to check if that was possible. Didn't even look that bad: just a strip of dirty water at the bottom of a four-foot concrete pipe.

But whenever I tried to get her to explore with me, she'd just call me Bug and give me a look.

This time, though, she followed as I snuck into the ditch across the street from the school and eyed the pipe. Cramped, dark, and damp. Still, I'm not saying the place smelled *pleasant*, but it wasn't that bad.

Anyway, I'd spent the night in the root canal. What was a little more mud?

We crept down the pipe, hunched over. We figured the fuse box was in the main janitorial closet, not too far from the basement.

All we needed to do was follow the pipe to the basement, climb the stairs and zip across the hall to the janitorial closet, and turn all the fuses off.

Easy, right?

Well, we got into the basement. And just like the school gossip said, the grate at the other end of the pipe was loose. We squeezed inside.

Then we climbed the stairs. So far so good.

Until we tried to open the door.

It was locked.

That's what I mean about having your plan fall apart. You think everything's going fine; then you run into a locked door.

Now, I don't know about you, but Jamie and I don't know how to pick locks or anything. They don't teach that in school—and even if they had, I probably would've gotten a C.

So we were stuck before we'd even started. Meanwhile,

in the auditorium, a hundred yards away, our town was being scanned into the VIRUS data banks. Including Jamie's parents.

Jamie ranted for a while and started kicking the door. I stopped her, though—afraid Roach's soldiers would hear—and she finally calmed down and sat beside me on the stairs.

And started to cry.

We sat there for a bit, and I couldn't think of anything to say, so I gave her a hug.

As my eyes adjusted to the dark, I looked around. I saw an aluminum ventilation shaft running across the basement, hanging just below the ceiling.

"You think that's air-conditioning?" I asked Jamie.

She looked. "I dunno."

"You think it'd support our weight?"

"Not sure."

"Would we even fit inside?"

"Probably not."

"Okay," I said, standing. "Sounds like we have a plan."

I dragged a desk over and stacked a bunch of milk crates on top. Then we climbed the crates, opened a grate, and squeezed inside.

A tight fit. But the vent didn't collapse. And we managed to worm our way forward.

We crawled into the maze of ventilation shafts, ready to save the day.

FUZZY, WAS HE?

The three security droids charged forward, robotic arms grasping and missile turrets swiveling.

"Poppy," Larkspur said, "you distract them. Play defense, though."

"My pleasure." She bounded forward with a series of acrobatic martial-arts moves. The droids fired and missed. She did a handspring off the nearest droid's head and flipped behind the three of them, trying to split them up.

"Cosmo, you take the uplink. I'll smash a—" Larkspur stopped and stared at Cosmo. "What do you think you're doing?"

Cosmo was winding the toy car he'd customized in Jamie's bedroom. "All work and no play makes Cosmo a dull boy."

He put the little toy car on the floor and it zoomed forward. When it reached the treads of the first droid, it burst open and spewed goop like an oil tanker hitting an iceberg. Slippery goop. Which coated the floor and immobilized the droids. They were spinning their wheels on a sheet of lubricant, unable to advance.

"Pretty good," Larkspur said.

"No, no." Cosmo shook his head. "You say, 'Now *that's* slick.'"

"Get Poppy and follow me."

"Because it's like an oil slick, see?"

Larkspur grunted, rammed a hole in the wall, and walked into the next room. He rammed a hole in another wall, leading to another room. Then he rammed a hole in a third wall and ended up in the Cray room.

"Instant hallway," he said. "Now let's jack out of here."

He turned to Poppy and Cosmo . . . but they weren't there.

They were still back in the first hallway, fighting the droids.

Poppy was having too much fun to leave. She'd figured out how to use her crowbar to disassemble the droids. She'd leap on top of one, ram the bar into a seam, and yank backward. Once she dug deep enough, she'd rip out a handful of wiring.

That did the trick.

Cosmo, meanwhile, decided he should practice his hand-to-hand skills. Just because he likes to play around with darts and toy cars doesn't mean he's not deadly in unarmed commando combat. So he spun and crouched in front of the first droid, dodging mini-missiles and electric pulses and exchanging blows with the robot arms.

Until suddenly:

Cosmo sort of . . . fuzzed for a second. His edges blurred and he seemed almost transparent. And when he returned to normal a moment later, he looked like he was stuck in slow motion.

Like he was moving underwater.

His agility and speed were half what they'd been, and the droid smashed him in the chest and aimed a missile at his head.

"Poppy," he yelled, "911!"

Poppy pivoted and leapt toward him. Then she fuzzed, too!

Right in middle of her leap. Instead of hitting the droid, she landed on a batch of the slippery goop, flipped head over tail a few times, and crashed into a wall.

The droids spun toward them. They were stuck on the slippery stuff, but they could still fire.

"I'd give my stripe for a rocket launcher right now," Cosmo said.

And the droid fired.

NO

I stared at the newest intersection of vents, which looked like every other intersection of vents.

"Which way?" I whispered.

"We came from over there." Jamie pointed. "Um. Didn't we?"

"I think I recognize that panel."

"The panels are all identical!" she said.

"Yeah, but . . ." I sighed. "We're lost."

"How about . . . that way?"

"Why not?"

We crawled through another intersection and heard Roach's voice.

"Next!" he called faintly.

And we knew that in the auditorium, another person had been scanned in.

We looked at each other and crawled toward the noise. Not just Roach's voice, but all the weeping and begging. We followed the sound into a vent leading to the auditorium.

Peering through a grate, we saw that the line in front of the scanning booth was smaller, with only a dozen people remaining. And Jamie's parents were almost in front.

"We have to do something," Jamie said.

"Let me think, let me think. . . ."

"We can find the fuse box and—"

"There's no *time*, Jamie," I hissed.

What could we do? Dozens of VIRUS soldiers. Plus Hund—who counted for dozens more all by himself. The auditorium was mostly empty now and strewn with trash and papers, a briefcase, a baseball glove . . .

Focus, Doug!

Roach still stood on the stage. Hund still wore a hundred pounds of killing machines. The glossy black scanning booth still looked like death.

But there, behind the booth: an uplink! Plugged into the scanning booth, like the booth couldn't work without it.

"If we can damage that uplink—" I started.

"Oh, no," Jamie said, her eyes wide. Her father was next in line.

We were too late.

"Next!" Roach called. And the soldiers shoved Jamie's dad into the machine.

The door shimmered. The booth hummed.

And he was gone.

"Oh no, oh no, oh no," Jamie said under her breath.

"Next!" Roach called.

They pushed Jamie's mother into the machine, and the door shimmered again.

"Noooooooo!" Jamie yelled as the booth digitized her mother.

The soldiers heard her. They looked up and saw the grate.

They sprang toward us.

SODA POP

An instant after the missile launched, a soda vending machine flew over Cosmo's head. It smashed into the missile and exploded into shrapnel and sugar water. Smoke billowed through the corridor, hiding the skunks.

Larkspur appeared at the end of the hallway, from where he'd thrown the soda machine. He grabbed Cosmo and Poppy, put one under each arm, and ran back toward the Cray room.

"You should've said, 'Have a Coke and a smile,'" Cosmo said from under Larkspur's arm.

"I told you to get Poppy," Larkspur said. "Not to play around with those droids."

"Not his fault," Poppy said.

"You should know better." Larkspur dropped Poppy and Cosmo on the ground of the Cray room a little harder than necessary. "Both of you."

They stood up and wiped themselves off. "Something happened," Poppy said. "We lost power."

"What?"

"We were doing fine; then we lost power."

Larkspur checked his wrist display. "It's starting. What Dr. Solomon warned us about. Dissolving into a bundle of information."

"You didn't feel it?" Poppy asked.

"Not yet. The suit has its own power source, so I can last longer than you. A little longer. Time to go."

Larkspur grabbed the uplink and flickered out of existence.

But the uplink stayed behind.

Big problem.

In a moment, Larkspur rematerialized. The other two skunks stared at him.

"Don't say it," Cosmo said. "I don't want to hear it."

"We can't do it. We can digitize ourselves, and a little extra, like our gear. But I can't digitize the uplink. It exceeds my capacity."

"I told you not to say it."

"So how do we get out of here?" Poppy asked. "And how do we get an uplink to Dr. Solomon?"

<Skunks>, my aunt said, broadcasting a message directly into the skunks' digital caches. <Come quickly. The children need help.>

<But, Dr. Solomon>, Larkspur replied. <We're having trouble with—>

<I can't maintain this connection. It's draining my resources. Jack in, and I will route you directly to the chil—>

And the connection died.

"Great," Cosmo said.

"I don't care if I *am* reverting to pure information." Poppy smiled her scary smile. "These colors don't run."

"You're not in color," Cosmo said. "You're black and white."

"This isn't about running," Larkspur told her. "We don't have time to play around. We have a duty to Dr. Solomon, we need to help the chi—"

CHUNG CHUNG CHUNG CHUNG CHUNG.

Larkspur stopped talking, and they all looked down the hallway.

The droids were back. And they'd brought friends.

HUMDRUM

The soldiers ripped the grate off the wall and grabbed us.

I'd go into detail about how they pulled us from the ventilation shaft as we tried to scramble away, but why bother? The truth is, they were soldiers and we were kids. We never had a chance.

"Bring them here," Roach said.

The soldiers shoved us forward.

Hund glowered at me. "How's your leg?"

Too scared to say anything clever—or even anything stupid, for that matter—I just stared at him.

He pulled his knife. "Remember this? My favorite blade?"

I swallowed hard.

Hund stepped closer and grabbed the front of my shirt. Then he lifted me three feet into the air.

I heard Jamie yell, "Let him go!"

Pretty impressive. I didn't feel like yelling anything except "Mommy!"

"I could do that," Hund said, and shook me. "Or I could snap him in half."

"Make him give you the Resloc first," Roach said.

"Gimme," Hund snarled at me.

"Um—" I swallowed. "I—I don't know w-what that is."

"The place where you downloaded a copy of the Protocol," Roach said. "Oh, yes, very clever. Did you think I wouldn't notice?"

"I d-don't know what you're t-talking about," I stammered.

And I didn't. Maybe if I hadn't been so bone-deep terrified, I'd have realized he meant the skunks. That was where the Protocol had been downloaded. But at that moment, I could barely remember how to breathe.

"Don't play with me, boy," Hund said.

He stared into my eyes, and I could see my reflection in his implanted yellow lens, and I looked scared.

He tightened his grip on me and brought his blade closer, and everything started to go black. I guess I was about to faint.

"I have it!" Jamie shouted. They all turned to her. "Don't hurt him. I know the Resloc."

"And who are *you*?" Hund sneered.

"I'm the girl who knows the Resloc number: 21c07lr84-84."

Roach cocked his head when she rattled off the numbers. "A child with a *brain*. How unusual." He tapped a few keys, then nodded in satisfaction. "You downloaded the Protocol into the test animals?"

"I guess," I said.

"A pity the animals were incinerated." He turned to Hund. "Everything is going perfectly. The scans were flawless; the first stage is complete. The digitization of a neighborhood. Next comes a small city, then a state. And then"—he smiled his freaky smile—"perfect order. Perfect logic."

"Stage one is complete?" Hund asked.

"Indeed. And nothing can—"

"Then it's time for my payment." Hund tossed me to the floor and I fell on my butt. "My upgrades."

"Patience, Commander."

"I want those—"

"I'll activate the upgrades when we return to base."

The soldier holding Jamie grabbed me, too. "What should I do with these two?"

"Toss them into the mix," Roach said, nodding at the scanning booth.

"Together?"

"Oh, yes. Quite an interesting experiment. Finish the ones in the queue; then add the children. They'll be our last two uploads."

THE GRUESOME TWOSOME

They scanned in the last few people. I'll skip over the crying, the screaming, the pleading. Then the soldier holding me and Jamie started dragging us forward, toward the scanning booth.

Jamie caught my eye and mouthed, *One, two . . . three!*

At exactly the same time, we both shoved and tugged and kicked and pulled, trying to get away.

No good. The soldier just scoffed and tossed us into the machine.

A moment later, the door shimmered closed.

Pitch-black. Not even a hint of light. And we were about to be scanned into Roach's world.

"Jamie?" I said.

"Right here," she answered, and took my hand.

The machine started to hum.

AND KNOW WHEN TO RUN

CHUNG CHUNG CHUNG CHUNG CHUNG: a dozen security droids advanced in a phalanx.

Poppy cartwheeled behind them and tore through armor with her crowbar while Cosmo blasted away with his stun guns. In a moment, four of the security droids were smoldering wrecks, but the rest kept attacking with mindless ferocity.

Then Poppy fuzzed, and a mini-missile exploded behind her shoulder. And when Cosmo fuzzed, too, a robot arm smashed him across the hall.

Larkspur stepped in to protect them from an electronic pulse, which shorted his circuitry. "We have to disengage!" he yelled, head-butting a droid into smithereens. "The children need us."

"Without the uplink?" Cosmo asked as he fired a volley of ball bearings.

"We have no other choice," Larkspur said.

"Not me," Poppy said. "I don't run from—"

As a missile flung her backward, she fuzzed again—her edges frayed even more. Another power-down. Another step closer to dissolving

into

a

bund1e

0f

pure

1nf0rmat10n . . .

"Jack in!" Larkspur roared. "The children are in danger, and this isn't a fight we can win."

The security droids launched a barrage of missiles.

Poppy dodged, Cosmo fired countermeasures, and Larkspur shrugged off the impact . . . but one missile struck home.

Direct hit on the uplink: the missile blasted it into a charred husk.

Completely destroyed. Now there were only *two* uplinks, and Roach had both.

DOESN'T FEEL LIKE VICTORY

Cold. Dark. The scent of fear. The feel of Jamie's hand in mine. The sound of the machine humming.

The end of everything.

And then, from outside the scanning machine, a familiar voice: "Now *this* is a fight we can win."

The darkness seemed to brighten.

"Cosmo," Jamie whispered. Then she yelled, "We're in here! Cut the power!"

I heard the sharp whistle of Poppy's chain, and the humming stopped with a sudden *crackle-ffzt*. Then someone screamed and thudded heavily to the ground.

"You threatened the children," Larkspur said, his deep voice suddenly unfriendly. "That was a mistake."

Gunfire sparked and a guard screamed. Bullets ricocheted and something exploded: *FWOOOM*.

Cosmo laughed. "You call *that* a grenade? No, no. *This* is a grenade."

FWOOOOOOM!

For about two minutes, screaming and gunfire and explosions echoed in the auditorium. Sounded like a full-scale war out there. Instead of being the last place on earth I wanted to be, the scanning booth suddenly seemed like a nice, safe hideout.

Then we heard Roach's voice: "Terminate encounter. Evacuate."

"No!" Hund yelled. "I can beat them."

"Perhaps," Roach said. "But I won't risk it. We have work to do. Evacuate."

A loud rumble came from all around us, and the booth trembled and shook. Felt like the auditorium walls were collapsing and the roof was falling in. Then the rumble grew fainter, moving away—Roach's evacuation vehicle—and a second later, the door opened.

Cosmo.

Jamie burst out and gave him a big hug. "Cosmo!"

"Owwwww!" he said.

"We have to get my paren—" Jamie started. Then she saw him, all his burns and cuts. And the other two skunks looked even worse. "We have to get you all to a hospital."

"A hospital can't help us," Larkspur said. "Only the uplink

can help us. Only the uplink can save Dr. Solomon."

"So where *is* it?"

The skunks looked glum standing there, backlit by the fires burning on the floor and the daylight streaming through the demolished ceiling.

"We lost it in the cross fire," Cosmo said. "We failed."

"How are we supposed to get an uplink now?" I asked in a whiny voice. "You'll revert, and my aunt'll fade into the Net. We're not just gonna stumble on an uplink. Unless . . ."

I stepped aside and gestured with a sort of triumphant flourish. There, behind the scanning machine, was the uplink I'd seen earlier.

Poppy's ears perked and Cosmo cheered and tossed me about ten feet into the air. Luckily, he caught me, too.

Larkspur grabbed the uplink. "Let's get this to Dr. Solomon without delay."

"To her where?" I asked. "She's in the Net."

"Jamie's laptop is the best conduit, synchronized with the—" Larkspur stopped. "Where *is* the laptop?"

"Um," I said. "Still in Jamie's bedroom."

He nodded. "Then let's have a Coke and smile."

I looked at him. *"What?"*

"Cosmo told me I should say that." His metal brow furrowed. "No?"

"No," I said, and we headed outside.

Halfway to the auditorium doors, I noticed Jamie lagging behind, looking around the now-empty room at the wreckage and the flames.

Her eyes sad and her head bowed in grief.

Maybe her mom and dad worked too many hours; maybe they gave her too many *things* and not enough time. Maybe they hardly saw her and didn't really know her—maybe they even called her princess sometimes.

But they loved her. And they were all the family she had.

Except me.

I stood beside her. "I'm sorry."

She nodded, biting her lip.

"I promise . . ."

"What?"

"We'll get them back. With the skunks on our side . . . we'll get them back."

"Yeah," she said.

I hope she believed me. But the truth was I wasn't so sure myself.

I didn't say anything else; I just walked beside her back to her house. The streets were empty. The town looked like a ghost town. The skunks kept watch from rooftops and telephone poles, but we walked straight to Jamie's house, and nobody tried to stop us.

I paused outside her front door, thinking about the family who'd lived there before Jamie. When I was a little kid, I used to spy on them with my aunt's binoculars, especially at dinnertime. Watching them together talking and laughing like the McCheerfuls from Planet Perfect, I'd feel a hot bubble of envy in my stomach.

Then Mr. and Mrs. McCheerful divorced.

I'd realized there was more to family than having a mom and dad, and vowed never to take Auntie M for granted again. And instead of being jealous, I'd always felt bad that Jamie only saw her parents a few hours a week.

Now she didn't even have that.

We crowded into Jamie's bedroom with the skunks, and Larkspur talked to my aunt for a few minutes, reconfiguring the uplink, while Jamie vanished into the house somewhere. Maybe her parents' room, I don't know.

When she returned, Larkspur asked her to check the configuration with her dragonfly. At first I thought he and Auntie M were just trying to keep Jamie occupied, to take her mind off her loss. But she fired up *CircuitBoard* and started muttering about codelinks and optimal routing, until finally they were satisfied.

"Here goes," Larkspur said, and vanished.

"How long's this gonna take?" I asked Jamie.

"Not sure. A minute or two." But she was distracted, chatting with Auntie M on the keyboard—typing a private conversation.

So I took the hint and crossed the room toward Poppy, who was lounging in Jamie's chair, brushing her tail and watching Cosmo tinker with an old CD player and some party supplies.

"I could've taken Hund," Poppy was saying.

"Sure," Cosmo said, pouring silver powder into deflated balloons. "I could tell by the way you kept hitting his fist with your face."

"Hund's not so tough. If I was at full power . . ."

"He's not human, I'll tell you that."

"Who isn't?" I asked. "Hund?"

"Born human," Cosmo said, "but someone's been messing with his code. He's genetically altered or something."

"Upgraded," I said. "That's what Roach said. Something about his upgrades."

"Well, next time we meet," Poppy said, "I'm gonna *down-grade* him."

Just then, Larkspur reanimated through the uplink.

"Much better," he said, his injuries gone and his armor repaired.

"My turn," Cosmo said, and digitized into the uplink.

He reappeared in two minutes, his cuts healed and a

dozen new devices on his belt and bandolier. Grappling hooks and flash grenades and smoke bombs, all small and brightly colored.

Maybe he really *had* spent too many iterations in *SimToys*.

Poppy raised an eyebrow at him. "Do any of those come in *black*?"

"We're black and white enough already."

"They look like toys."

"For the element of surprise," he said. "There's no better way to make an adversary underestimate you."

"And . . . ?" Larkspur said, prompting him.

Cosmo looked a little abashed. "And I like 'em colorful."

Poppy snorted, but I saw a glint in her eyes in the instant before she digitized. And when she reanimated, she had not only a new, longer motorcycle chain but throwing stars.

Yet she grumbled unhappily.

"What's wrong?" I asked.

"No Harley," she said.

"We can't download objects that size," Larkspur said. "The weight limitations are fairly stringent. The algorithm, if you're interested, is—"

"I'm not," Poppy said, still scowling.

"The only thing I wanna download," I said, "is my aunt."

The skunks turned to Jamie, who was still sitting at the computer, tapping on the keyboard. For a moment, nobody spoke:

nobody wanted to interrupt her conversation after what had just happened to her parents.

"Pardon me, Jamie," Larkspur finally said.

Jamie looked up. "Mm?"

"We're not sure how to configure the uplink for Dr. Solomon."

"Oh," she said, and glanced at me.

"What?" I asked.

"Um," she said. "The thing is, Doug . . ."

"Let me explain," Auntie M said through the computer speakers. "I've been scanning the information Jamie downloaded from Roach's site."

"Did you get a lock on his base?" Poppy asked.

"Not yet." The hard drive spun, then quieted. "However, I'm stunned by his technical advances. Those scanning booths are frightening. He really is evil—and he really is brilliant."

"An evil genius," Cosmo murmured. "Excellent."

"Plus the attack on the auditorium . . . ," my aunt continued. "Scanning in hundreds of people . . . He's even more of a threat than I'd realized."

"That's why we need his home address," Poppy said. "End the threat once and for all."

"During my conversation with the new Awareness—" my aunt started.

"You spoke to it?" I asked.

"To *her*," my aunt said. "Yes."

"Her? The computer is a she?"

"The Awareness is me, Doug. That 'corrupted' data emerged from my brain. I am me, and the Awareness is also me. Mostly. But she's better integrated into the Net; she won't lose integrity. She will never dissolve."

"What about you? Can't you reanimate through the uplink?"

"Yes, I . . ." She paused. "I *could*, Doug."

"But?"

"But I won't."

"What are you talking about?"

"I'm sorry, Doug. I'm so sorry."

"Sorry for *what*?" I looked at Jamie. "What is she saying?"

Jamie just shook her head, her eyes big and sad.

"Here are the facts," my aunt said. "Roach is more powerful than I imagined. His software is generations beyond what I expected, both the scanning technology and the biodigital weapons he's developing. He's a threat to the entire country. The entire world."

"Yeah, I got that," I said. "Reanimate, and we'll fight him together."

"No one knows about him but us, Doug. The skunks are the only weapon that can touch him—they can fight in both reality and virtual reality. They can switch back and forth without an uplink. They're our only hope."

"Uh-huh."

"And the Awareness projects that cybercriminal activity and the virtual underworld are going to explode."

I shook my head. "You mean like credit card fraud? Who cares?"

"I mean a crime wave like nothing we've ever seen."

"But what about *you*, Auntie M? What about *you*?"

"If I reanimate," she said, "the Awareness will cease to exist."

"But you will—*you'll* exist."

"I'm going to stay on the Net, Doug," my aunt said. "I'll merge with the Awareness to fight VIRUS and—"

"You're leaving me. You promised you'd always be there—and now you're leaving and you're not coming back."

"I—"

"You'll die," I said.

"No," she said. "But I *will* change. I will be part myself, and part data network. Yet as long as VIRUS is a threat . . . I have no choice. Once I merge with the Awareness, I can monitor Roach. It's the only chance we have."

I stormed away and slammed the door behind me.

AND WASH BEHIND MY EARS

Jamie found me in the guest room five minutes later.

"Bug?" she said.

"Go away."

She sat beside me on the bed.

If she said anything, I was gonna scream. I knew that Auntie M didn't have a choice—of course she had to fight Roach. And I knew that Jamie had just lost her parents to Roach's cyber domain.

But I'd already lost my parents. I *needed* Auntie M.

Maybe that makes me selfish, but . . . sometimes I thought I was cursed. They call me Bug because things break down around me. I didn't care about that.

But what if *people* broke down around me, too?

My aunt, Jamie's parents. My whole town. My mother and father.

But Jamie didn't say anything. She just sat there beside me. And after a while, I felt better. Having a friend like her—at least *that* didn't break down.

Finally, I turned to her and said, "Thanks."

She smiled a little sadly. "I needed that, too."

"I'm sorry about your mom and dad. You know Auntie M— or *whatever*—will try everything to get them back."

"I know." She touched my arm. "That's one reason she's . . .

merging, I think. Joining with this Awareness, or whatever. For me. To try to help me."

"Yeah, I figured."

"You're not mad?"

I shook my head. "Not at you."

She squeezed my hand. "What are we going to do?"

"Fight," I said. "Fight until we get your parents back. Until we get *everyone* back."

HELP

That's why I started this blog: because we can't do this alone, we can't win without help. Without *you*. Act as our eyes and ears. Watch for Roach and VIRUS, and don't believe the lies. Stay alert, stay focused—stay sharp.

Now you know about the skunks. Yeah, they're ridiculous, but they're also real and the most powerful weapon we have. The most advanced biodigital life-forms on the planet.

But Roach? He's getting stronger every day—every minute—expanding his domain and creating new weapons.

We got the uplink from the auditorium. We stabilized the skunks. My aunt could've regenerated . . . but fighting VIRUS was more important. I'm not gonna pretend I'm happy about that, but she didn't have any choice.

We're in this fight together. Me and Jamie. Auntie M—or whatever's left of her. The skunks.

And you.

BORDER PATROL

After Jamie and I talked for a while, we headed back to her bedroom.

"It's done," Larkspur told me as we stepped inside. For a guy in a deadly combat suit, he sure had kind eyes.

"Auntie M?" I asked.

"I am here," said the voice from the computer.

"Is it really you?"

Random images flashed on the screen: train tracks, a hummingbird, mathematical equations, a palm tree. "I have integrated with the Awareness and transformed it."

I swallowed and didn't say anything. Because that didn't sound like Auntie M.

"And she has transformed me, too," the voice continued. "I am still me, Doug—just a slightly *different* me."

"In what way?" Larkspur asked, hunched over Jamie's laptop.

"My mind is spread throughout cyberspace, running thousands of operations at any given moment, monitoring tens of thousands of channels. I do not see through eyes or hear through ears; instead, I patch into security cameras and cell phones and electrical outlets. I am like the Center's AI, but I have several new parameters of concern." The pictures on the screen started flickering too fast to recognize. "For example, I am concerned that Douglas does not eat a sufficient quantity of vegetables to maintain optimal health."

I gave a feeble laugh, partly from stress, and partly from relief that Auntie M was still in there somewhere. Maybe she wasn't reanimating completely; maybe she wasn't gonna walk through the door. Maybe she wasn't gonna sit across from me for dinner or wake me in the morning with a hockey stick to the ribs.

But she wasn't dead, either. She wasn't gone forever; she hadn't left me completely. I guess I found that pretty comforting.

Then we got down to business. The first thing was Jamie's parents.

"Are they hurt?" Jamie asked.

"They feel no pain," my cyber aunt told her. "Roach's scans do not allow higher consciousness."

"So . . . they can't *think*?"

"They simply know that they must perform their function. Expand Roach's virtual world. Although . . ."

"What?" Poppy said.

"I've reviewed the files Jamie downloaded from the Resloc." Images blurred on the screen: snowflakes, cartoons, scientific notation. "Once he perfects the technology, Roach intends to implant new memories and goals above the ones that already exist. And then to reanimate the subjects."

"So he'll brainwash them?" Larkspur asked. "And then output them?"

"They will appear precisely the same, but inside will be merely components of Roach's program."

"Perfect spies," Cosmo said. "And if he can replicate powerful people . . ."

"You mean like scan in the president?" I asked. "Then mess with his mind and output him again?"

"Exactly," Auntie M said.

"But I thought Roach wanted to destroy the world, not take over."

"This is just a first step, Doug. Once he controls the politicians and the generals, the celebrities and newscasters, then he'll have no trouble scanning everything he wants into his servers. And once he's done, he'll destroy all life on earth. He'll destroy everything but his computers, humming away in underground bunkers. Still, he's a long way from perfecting that technology."

"Let's not wait until he does," Larkspur said. "We need to save those people he scanned."

"So we attack?" Poppy sounded eager.

"She'd beat *herself* up," Cosmo muttered, "just for something to do."

"I've discovered Roach's weakness," my aunt said. "With Jamie's help."

Jamie smiled, though her eyes still looked sad. "All of Roach's data is currently saved to a single server, to escape detection. After we download the minds of his victims—to keep them safe—we can destroy the server and he's finished."

"Though we don't have much time," Auntie M said.

"Yeah, he's gonna transfer everything to a secure domain," Jamie said. "Once he does that, his data will be completely protected."

Larkspur nodded. "So we attack before that happens."

"Just point and click me to him," Poppy said. "Where's this server?"

"We need to raid his server to find out."

"What?" Cosmo said. "We have to what his what to what?"

Jamie spoke a little more slowly. "Raid his *virtual* server to find his real one."

"I'm with Cosmo," I said. "That doesn't make sense."

"Roach's virtual world is generated by real computers," Auntie M said as a starburst of images appeared on the screen. "We need to invade his virtual domain. From there, we can determine his real-world location."

"Sounds like a job for the bug," Cosmo said.

"Hey!" I said.

"I meant Jamie's bug," he said. "The dragonfly."

"You are partially correct," my aunt said. "Jamie and Doug can track the information through the *CircuitBoard* interface on her laptop."

"How can they get through Roach's defenses?"

"That's not just any laptop—it's hub-upgraded and Protocol-enhanced. And you skunks will be there to protect them."

"From what? Power surges?"

"Cyberdroids. Roach has been busy."

CYBER-WHA?

We buzzed along the "ground," rocketing past file structures and directory guides.

Well, actually, we—Jamie and I—sat in her bedroom, staring at the computer. Jamie controlled the dragonfly and we saw the virtual world through its eyes.

Bizarre.

This was still the regular Net, though—we hadn't reached Roach's domain yet—so nothing was too exciting.

With one exception. One tiny exception.

On the computer screen, the skunks raced alongside the dragonfly.

They looked exactly like they did in real life, except surrounded by information swirls and data flows. Jamie told me that they're completely digital inside the computer, but her laptop translated them into graphics, down to the last detail: the gleam of Larkspur's armor, the triggers on Cosmo's guns, the studs on Poppy's leather jacket.

For the first time in forever, I almost relaxed. *This* I understood. Something finally made sense. Because looking at Jamie's laptop, I saw a video game. And this one had weapons.

We approached Roach's domain and slowed. The skunks checked their gear. Jamie wiped her hand and changed her grip on the joystick. And we went in.

The transformation blew my mind.

In the time since Roach had scanned in the people from our town, everything had changed. They'd been slaving away for him—each scanned person as powerful as a supercomputer with an advanced AI—working together like an ant colony building a massive hive, with tunnels and mounds and chambers.

Of course, they weren't really building tunnels and mounds and chambers. That's just how the laptop depicted the objects. Really they were building code, expanding Roach's domain, expanding his power.

But everything looked . . . *real*.

Impossible, but real.

Imagine an endless cartoonish assembly plant—and we're talking horror cartoons, not Saturday morning—where the laws of physics didn't work and pure information ruled.

Okay, this isn't going to make much sense, but I watched things—impossible shapes with shifting colors—carried by conveyor belts into bizarre machines and transformed into new, different things.

Everything combining, expanding, condensing, mushrooming. Everything tWeAKed, everything

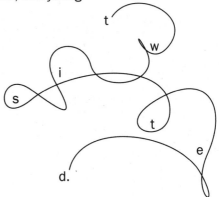

Including the people. Oh, they looked a little like people—two legs, two arms, and a head. But Roach hadn't given them features.

No faces. No eyes, no mouth.

You know those balloon animals that clowns make? Imagine people who look like that. I'd never seen anything so frightening.

You think being chased by an ax murderer is a nightmare? Or falling from an airplane? Or drowning? This was worse.

Way worse.

Despite being faceless, these were real people—my friend Mason, Letitia Harrod, Stacy Nguyen, Jamie's parents—slaving away in a virtual sweatshop, their free will deleted. Real people reduced to identical cogs in a digital machine, increasing the power of the madman who'd reduced them to this.

I felt clammy sweat on the back of my neck. "That's . . ."

"Horrible," Jamie finished. And I knew she was thinking about her parents.

On the screen, the skunks seemed to be sniffing the digital "wind."

Then Poppy pointed and said, "The origin's that way."

Jamie took a breath. She tapped the joystick, giving a little waggle of the dragonfly's wings to say thanks, and zoomed off.

We whizzed through the factory, through cyber gears and over data storage tanks and around code blocks. Poppy and Cosmo raced alongside—I couldn't see Larkspur—ready to jump in if things got dangerous.

Jamie sped around, testing the dragonfly's capabilities. And, to be honest, sightseeing. Because Roach's realm was pretty incredible. Not beautiful, not inviting, but truly amazing.

Which is why we didn't notice it at first.

The cyberdroid.

Something flickered on the edge of the screen.

"There!" I said.

Jamie turned the dragonfly to look—and even though we were just watching on the monitor, we screamed.

A creature with razor fangs and flayed skin and too many arms rose from the digital ground. It mutated as we watched. Skin melted and re-formed, claws curved and glinted.

"What on earth—" Jamie said.

A slimy tentacle shot toward the dragonfly, and the droid sprang forward.

Jamie didn't stick around. She jerked the joystick, hitting full power and taking evasive action: twisting and twirling the dragonfly in cyberspace, trying to escape the droid.

No luck. That thing was coded to do exactly this—hunt and destroy.

Jamie zoomed into an alley between two sheer digital walls, then flew straight up some kind of hollow shaft. But the droid immediately grew tree-frog toes to climb the vertical surfaces, then oozed through tiny cracks into the shaft. It never stopped and never slowed.

Still, Jamie was no slouch. She faked the dragonfly right, then darted left and dove into a series of deep, narrow ditches and followed them at breakneck speed.

"Where are the skunks?" she said through gritted teeth.

"You lost them at that first corner," I told her.

She grunted and pulled the dragonfly into a roll, maneuvering between a tangle of cyber cables.

But eventually it had to happen. She just wasn't fast enough.

A thick wad of something gross flew out of the cyberdroid's mouth and plastered the dragonfly to the wall.

"I can't move," Jamie said, biting her lip. "Maybe if I bypass the circuitry . . ."

She typed fast—frantically—trying her *CircuitBoard* magic. But there was no time.

The cyberdroid loped closer to the dragonfly and squatted on its haunches. It spat another wad at us, then leaned forward and stared.

"It's no good," Jamie said. "I can't get away."

"Look at its eyes."

At first they'd appeared a blank white that somehow shone with malice—but now computer code scrolled inside the eye sockets.

"It's tracing us," Jamie said. "Roach is using the droid as a probe. He'll hack the dragonfly code and find—"

"How cool is *that*?" Cosmo's voice came through the speakers. "It spits!"

We couldn't see him on the screen, but apparently the cyber-droid could. It launched upward and spun in midair, extending a dozen claws, ready for attack.

"How come Roach's creatures get all the best toys?" Cosmo said.

"You want a phlegm-shooter?" Poppy asked. She flashed onto the screen, flying through the air, and landed a kick on the cyberdroid's shoulder.

The droid howled and twisted, bounced off a data grid, and returned the attack.

For a moment, Poppy and the cyberdroid exchanged blows faster than the eye could see.

Cosmo ran forward, and we finally saw him on the screen. He'd somehow generated a whole new batch of weapons.

In cyberspace, I am able to provide Cosmo with most of the gear he requests. I am able to provide the same service to Poppy, incidentally, which explains—

Right, of course.

In addition to her new chain, Poppy had a new crowbar strapped to her right leg and her throwing stars strapped to her left. Plus a new leather jacket, with spikes and chains. And biker boots, of course.

Cosmo was in full commando gear, with camouflage, holsters, and a flak jacket. He was holding what looked like a Ping-Pong ball gun, and his bandoleer was full of brightly colored gadgets.

He raced along a railing, then flipped into the air, past the cyberdroid, and landed with his gun ready.

"Get your own playmate," Poppy told him, blocking a blow to her head. "I saw it first."

Cosmo wavered for a second, then holstered his gun. "Sheesh, you get all the fun."

Then the cyberdroid sprouted another arm, which grabbed Poppy by the neck and started squeezing.

"Hey!" She twisted and slashed the droid's arm with her jacket spikes. "It's growing arms."

The droid shrieked and recoiled.

"The better to hug you with," Cosmo said, and fired.

His gun looked silly and lightweight and harmless. But he'd modified the firing mechanism—those balls fired hard enough to stun a rhino—and he'd customized the ammo, too.

The ball shot toward the cyberdroid's head, and the droid dodged and lashed at Cosmo with its spiked tail.

Yeah, its tail. That thing grew new limbs in the blink of a cursor.

Cosmo spun away and yelled, "Flash!"

Poppy pulled her jacket over her eyes.

Jamie and I didn't know what was going on—and neither did the cyberdroid—until the Ping-Pong ball burst open with a tremendous flash of light.

On Jamie's monitor, it was incredibly bright. In virtual reality, it was blinding.

Literally. The droid clutched its eyes and screamed. I don't know how long the blindness would've lasted, but—

Everything in virtual reality is based on digital code. Hence Cosmo's flash balls affect the underlying format of the droid's sensors, not actual eyes. The duration of the effect depends on the type of sensor it is utilized against.

Oh, sure. What she said.

Anyway, Poppy finished off the blinded droid in a few seconds. A couple of throwing stars, and the droid dissolved into a heap of digital information.

Which looked a lot like bar codes melting in a pile of sludge.

Cosmo crossed to the dragonfly, pulled a knife from his boot sheath, and chopped at the gunk that plastered the dragonfly to the wall.

"This stuff is gross," he said, obviously impressed. "Cyber drool."

Where's Larkspur? Jamie typed. She couldn't talk directly through the dragonfly, but the skunks could "hear" her when she typed.

"Doing some research," Poppy said. "Him and Dr. Solomon are checking into . . . upgrades, I think. So you've only got two bodyguards."

Upgrades? I typed. *Is this about Hund?*

"I wasn't listening. Too busy sharpening my throwing stars."

"Great," I muttered.

Cosmo freed the dragonfly and Jamie warily tested the controls.

"Still working?" I asked.

She smiled. "Perfectly."

Then she typed, *Can you get a read on the information flow?*

Poppy sniffed, then pointed to her left. "We're downstream from a vast data source. Try that way."

"Roach's server?" I asked.

"Gotta be," Jamie said.

"Look at this." Cosmo showed Poppy a chunk of the cyberdroid spit in his hand. "This stuff is amazing. Self-regenerating, and—ooooof!"

Three dark, jagged shapes had shot onto the screen, and one caught Cosmo in the stomach and flung him backward. Two flew at Poppy, but her crowbar was out in a flash, her reflexes video-game fast, and she deflected the shapes.

"Cosmo? Are you all right?"

Cosmo backflipped to his feet. "What *was* that? Some kind of automated defense—" Then he yelled a warning: "Poppy!"

Before she could react, Poppy was lifted ten feet in the air and smashed back into the ground.

The cyberdroid had regenerated. Twice as big, twice as

fast, and twice as ugly. Drooling jaws opened, a wad of spit shot at Cosmo, and the droid lunged forward to crush him. At the same time, it spun Poppy with its two tails—yeah, now it had two—and smashed her into a nearby cylinder.

Cosmo dove aside and rolled, pulling a bright red beanbag from his bandoleer.

"Ever play Hacky Sack?" he asked.

He drop-kicked the beanbag at the droid and in the same motion drew his gun and flicked a switch, choosing which ball he'd shoot. This time he wasn't messing around with a flash ball; he selected the serious artillery.

He took aim and—

A second cyberdroid roared from behind him and fired a dozen blades at his back.

Cosmo dodged, looking like an Olympic gymnast, and yelled, "Jamie! Get out of here! Now! Go!"

We went.

BECAUSE MY JAW ACHES FROM YAWNING

Jamie flew the dragonfly at full power, keeping low, keeping out of sight. Staying in shadows and behind cover.

Moving fast.

"Where are you going?" I asked.

"If Poppy's right, the data's coming from this direction."

"How about that?" I pointed to an ominous structure at the top of the screen.

"That's a music playlist."

"Oh," I said, eyeing the grim shape. "Someone needs to lighten up."

"Shh," she said, trying to focus.

"Or maybe two someones," I muttered.

The dragonfly darted around a glowing cactus thing, and Jamie said, "There."

A flat black surface etched with signs and symbols, like a cave painting.

"That's Roach's server?"

"No." She guided the dragonfly toward the wall and started manipulating the symbols. "That's a window he forgot to lock."

She connected one symbol to another, twisted a third, and solved a fourth, faster than I could follow. Then, suddenly, the dragonfly reared backward, and I saw a new shape, one she'd created: a swirling spiral.

Jamie aimed at the spiral and charged full speed ahead. On the screen, the dragonfly went right *into* the spiral and through the wall.

We came out the other side in a tunnel. Not a regular tunnel—this tunnel slithered and spun around us. Imagine being inside a garden hose and shooting toward the nozzle . . . while someone used the hose as a jump rope.

"I've got to stay inside the conduit," Jamie said, jerking the joystick back and forth. "Or we'll get kicked out of the system."

Let me just say this: if I play *Smash and Grab III* with Jamie, I absolutely destroy her. Same with *HARP* and *Arsenal Five*. I bury her deep and feast on her bones.

Still, as far as staying in the conduit goes, she completely kicks butt. I felt a little jealous. All I was doing was watching, and here she was playing a video game for real.

Of course, she couldn't shoot anything, so I didn't care *that* much.

Anyway, she guided the dragonfly through the garden hose—or the conduit—for what seemed like forever but was probably only a minute or two. Then the dragonfly burst into a huge room, crisscrossed with energy pulses and direwire.

Oh, and the far side of the room was a wall of fire.

Coming closer. Fast.

"The firewall," Jamie said. "This is where it gets interesting."

Geez, silly me. Here I thought it already *was* interesting.

SKUNK ON A STICK

Cosmo leapt behind a cable car thing for cover, switching his gun to full automatic. But the second cyberdroid was smart. As Cosmo took aim, it oozed into the floor and disappeared. Cosmo heard a slithering and popping underground but couldn't get a shot on the droid.

Meanwhile, the first droid—the one attacking Poppy—looked in pretty rough shape. Cosmo's red beanbag had slammed its shoulder, split open, and poured tiny white beads all over.

Those were no ordinary beads. They were software irritants, like virtual poison ivy. They burrowed under the droid's skin and itched like crazy.

The droid stopped attacking Poppy to scratch. Not for long—just one brief second.

Which was all Poppy needed.

She cartwheeled to a ledge above the droid, lashed her chain around its neck, and squeezed. The droid bucked beneath her and fled in a panic, with Poppy still attached and pulling the chain tighter and tighter.

The droid zoomed past the other end of the virtual block, where Cosmo had bounded onto the cable car to buy a little time in case his droid erupted at him from underground.

That was exactly what the droid was waiting for: a pulse of

electricity surged through the cable and blasted Cosmo to the ground.

Then the droid rose in front of him, fifteen feet high, looking like a cross between a mutant octopus and a food processor. Its eight arms were covered with sucking pores and spinning blades, and its beak was huge and razor-sharp.

"Polly wanna cracker?" Cosmo flipped onto his feet and pulled the trigger.

A stream of balls poured from his gun, blasting a tentacle to shreds, exploding against the droid's leathery midsection. The droid staggered backward, then shimmered, code streaming inside its vacant white eyes.

Decoding Cosmo's ammo. Absorbing the ammo and gaining power. Growing larger and stronger.

"No more crackers for you," Cosmo said, spinning the dial on his gun again.

The droid slithered forward, as fast as a cobra and twice as venomous.

Cosmo aimed, a grin tugging at his muzzle. When the droid absorbed *these*, it'd be in for a shock. And then—

He dropped his gun and clutched his stomach.

At the spot where the jagged shape had slammed him earlier, his body froze solid. First his stomach, then his legs, then his shoulders and arms.

Completely motionless. Completely defenseless.

"Well, *this* is embarrassing," he said.

WITH A BATTERING RAM

So there we were. All that remained between us and the fire-wall—an avalanche of digital flames—was fifteen layers of virtual vectors and security schematics.

Sounds neat, right?

Wrong.

Jamie linked the positive and negative ports, aligned the modulators, assembled the sequential ports, and blah blah blah.

I'd enjoyed all the flying around but this part was *booooor-ing*. I mean, I guess *Jamie* was interested, but I'd rather watch televised bowling.

Anyway, the firewall approached.

Jamie typed.

I twiddled my thumbs.

Then we slipped past the firewall, into Roach's real-world server.

"Now what?" I asked.

"Now get me a soda from downstairs."

"Or I could ask you another hundred times."

She sighed. "Now I find the Resloc address and track the routing to a real-world origination point."

"You mean you search for Roach's address?"

She nodded. "Which will be a lot easier without you looking over my shoulder, complaining about how bored you are."

Fair enough.

"You want something to eat, too?" I asked.

She didn't answer, too busy with *CircuitBoard*.

I went downstairs to the kitchen and popped a frozen pizza into the oven, sat at the table for a second, then wandered into the living room. Felt strange, knowing her parents weren't coming home. Worse than strange.

The same with my house, I guessed. My aunt was gone. Where was I going to live? Tucked into a hard drive with my cyber aunt?

Maybe I wasn't bored, not really. Maybe I was just grieving—and scared. For as long as I could remember, Auntie M had been there: the most reliable person in my world. And now she'd turned herself into a stranger. Into something that wasn't even completely human.

And it wasn't just her I was grieving for. I needed to say good-bye to everything I'd ever known. My house, my street, my school. And we couldn't stay in town, obviously. "Town" didn't really exist anymore, and I wasn't gonna stick around and wait for Hund to knock on my front door.

But I didn't have any relatives. Jamie did, though. Her uncle Charlie and aunt Simone were probably the closest to her. I'd met them a couple of times. They weren't her mom and dad or anything, but they seemed okay.

They lived a thousand miles away, though. What if she moved in with them, and I . . . I dunno. Got left behind?

Flopping onto the couch, I turned on the TV and clicked through some soap operas, then paused at the news. They were talking about the explosion, but of course they didn't mention Roach or Hund or even the Center, and they kept saying a juvenile delinquent caused the whole mess.

And you know exactly who they were calling a juvie, don't you?

They had cops and ministers and psychologists all diagnosing me, explaining exactly what had gone wrong: my family and my brain and my morals, apparently. I couldn't wait to hear what they'd say once they learned how much I played video games.

I reached for the remote when I heard: "Tragedy at a local school." The newscaster looked solemn. "Hundreds are missing in what authorities are calling the most puzzling mass disappearance they've ever encountered."

The TV flashed to a reporter outside my school.

"This morning, in the auditorium you see behind me," the reporter said, "hundreds of people attended a town meeting about yesterday's explosion at a nearby medical research agency. But they never came out."

The cameras showed the inside of the auditorium. Empty. Trashed.

"How did these people vanish? Is this related to yesterday's explosion? As of now, only one person connects the two events." She frowned. "Authorities believe that Douglas Solomon, the only suspect in yesterday's explosion, was in this auditorium today—and now he is missing, presumably with the hundreds of other people."

Wonderful. I guess Roach fed the media that story so nobody would come looking once Hund got his hands on me.

Double wonderful.

I wondered if Roach and Hund knew about Jamie. If they'd identified her back in the auditorium. I hoped not. If she was lucky, she could still settle down to a semi-normal life with her aunt and uncle.

Which reminded me: I hadn't brought her that soda yet. I grabbed one and headed upstairs. On the way, I glanced out the window—and my heart nearly stopped.

Three army jeeps were speeding down the street toward Jamie's house! They leapt the curb and drove onto her front lawn.

I raced upstairs and burst into Jamie's room. "They're outside! They found us."

Jamie didn't even flinch. "That cyberdroid tracked us through the dragonfly." She snapped her laptop closed. "Where are they?"

Right then, the soldiers smashed through the front door.

"Does that answer your question?" I grabbed Jamie's hand and pulled her into the hallway.

SHUT YOUR TRAP

Poppy rode the cyberdroid like a bronco, using her motorcycle chain as reins.

The droid spun and shuddered but she stayed mounted, pulling the chain chokingly tight. The droid grew new arms to pluck her off its back, but couldn't reach. It grew a new tail. Still couldn't reach.

So it ran.

Imagine a roller coaster blasting full speed ahead—too fast to even breathe. Pulling loop-de-loops, rising high, then plunging down, whipping from left to right. Now imagine that the roller coaster is alive and trying to scrape you off its back, crashing through walls, slamming you into sharp edges and overhangs.

The ride of a lifetime. And Poppy shouted . . . in glee. This was her kind of fight: no rules, no tricky weapons. Just one-on-one with a creature three times her size.

She pulled her chain tighter, straining to sever the droid's neural network, her muzzle drawn back in a fierce smile.

And somehow, she won. Still, she was bruised and limping when she turned the corner and saw Cosmo frozen in place, with an even bigger cyberdroid poised to suck his digital guts out.

She moved her hands so fast they blurred. Her throwing stars sliced through the air, and in a microsecond, the droid was down to five tentacles.

"Ever consider a career as a sushi chef?" Cosmo asked. Then he yelled, "Watch out!"

Poppy dodged as two jagged shapes—the same things that had gotten Cosmo earlier—darted overhead.

"Those're nasty," Cosmo said. "They locked up my processing core."

Before Poppy could answer, the droid shot a barrage of blades at her. She spun away, but the droid anticipated her movements and body-slammed her into Cosmo. She knocked him onto his side, then sprang at the droid, crowbar flashing.

Behind her, Cosmo looked like a mannequin toppled on a department store floor, his body paralyzed and only his mouth able to move. And to complain: "Larkspur chose a great time to go researching with Dr. Solomon."

Then one of his ears perked. There, an inch in front of his muzzle: his gun!

He couldn't quite reach the grip with his mouth. So he stuck his tongue out and licked the gun closer, a centimeter at a time.

Meanwhile, the droid grew tentacles until nothing was visible but a writhing mass of limbs. Poppy sliced and kicked, and one last jagged shape flew at her from the depths of cyberspace.

Direct hit. Right between her shoulder blades.

"You've been hit!" Cosmo called. "Get to a datalink and jack us out before you get statuefied."

"Statuefied?"

"Jack out! You're already freezing up."

Between Poppy's shoulder blades, a small inertial field started rapidly growing. She cocked her head, then grabbed a nearby datalink and raced toward Cosmo.

She'd almost reached him when the cyberdroid leapt in front of her.

Poppy hesitated. She couldn't fight the droid and jack out at the same time.

And in a few seconds, she'd be frozen solid, too!

CHUTE 'EM UP

"Great plan," Jamie whispered.

"Shh," I said.

"What do we do now?"

"Shh," I said again.

My plan wasn't *that* bad. Just a little . . . incomplete.

When the soldiers burst in downstairs, we needed a place to hide. So I'd grabbed Jamie's hand and dragged her into the bathroom.

To the laundry chute. We didn't have one in my house, but at Jamie's, this chute ran from the upstairs bathroom to the washer and dryer in the basement. Toss your dirty socks into the hamper upstairs and find them waiting in a basket beside the washing machine.

So we squeezed in, slid down fifteen feet, then stopped, wedged inside.

Kinda wrapped around each other. A little too close for comfort.

I mean, Jamie and I are like brother and sister. When we text, she sometimes signs off with *LYLAB, Love You Like a Brother*. And I never *start* that, but I always answer *LYLAS*.

Except, um, she's not *actually* my sister. And, um . . . well. We were kinda smooshed together, like we were slow-dancing in a sleeping bag. So. Anyway. Um.

Where was I?

Oh, right: my plan was incomplete, but being stuck in the laundry chute kinda worked. The soldiers searched upstairs and didn't find us, then searched through the house and in the basement and still didn't find us.

"Kids don't disappear that easy," one said below us.

"These kids do."

"We should smoke 'em out."

The second soldier grunted. "Get the thermal scope."

"Yeah. If they still have body temperature, that'll find them."

Then we heard them clumping upstairs to the first floor.

"The thermal scope?" Jamie whispered.

"Quick!" I said. "Think cold thoughts."

She gave me a dirty look.

"Okay," I said. "They're gone. We'll slip into the basement and sneak out the window."

So we wiggled and squirmed but couldn't get unstuck. One problem was Jamie's laptop. The other problems were her elbow and her butt.

"Drop the laptop," I said, because expecting her to drop her butt seemed unrealistic.

"No."

"It's not gonna do us any good if those soldiers catch us. Drop it."

"No."

We squirmed some more. Somehow Jamie's forehead ended up whacking my nose. Probably on purpose.

"Ow! Drop it!"

"No!"

"You're crazy. Why not?"

"The dragonfly is localized to this machine. If I lose the laptop, I lose the dragonfly."

"Stupid thing can't even shoot," I muttered.

Jamie tried to punch me, and that did the trick. We were loose, falling through the laundry chute.

"Ooooooof!"

We landed on a heap of laundry in the basement. A few seconds later, we were on our feet. We ran to the side window and squirmed out.

Fast, quiet, efficient. Pretty darn good.

Except for one tiny problem.

The soldiers were waiting for us, one of them watching the house with what must've been the thermal scope.

"Have a nice ride?" he asked.

The other soldiers grabbed us from behind.

AND LOOK BOTH WAYS BEFORE CROSSING THE STREET

Poppy's tail lashed from side to side, a sure sign that she was angry. The freeze took the top of her body first, so she couldn't even talk—and she could barely stay on her feet.

The cyberdroid writhed toward her like a mutant octopus, barbed beak opening wide. Closer, closer . . . then suddenly letting loose a tremendous squawk.

No one knows much about the inner life of cyberdroids, but I think that squawk was a laugh. If cyberdroids feel anything, that one was feeling evil amusement.

At least, until Cosmo finally pulled the trigger with his tongue.

Cosmo insists that his training as an elite commando prepared him for this moment. I say it was pure luck.

Either way, while the droid was squawking at Poppy, one Ping-Pong ball arced through the air and flew right down its throat.

The cyberdroid shut its beak, widened its eyes, and exploded.

Very messy.

"And *that*," Cosmo said, "is why you shouldn't take candy from strangers."

Poppy, with the last bit of strength left in her legs, dragged the datalink to Cosmo. They focused for a second. Flickered.

And jacked out of there.

DO NOT PASS GO

Handcuffed again.

This time, in the back of a military truck driving away from home, with Jamie beside me and three soldiers guarding us like we were the FBI's most wanted instead of two scared kids.

Of course, it's possible we *were* the FBI's most wanted.

"Where are you taking us?" Jamie asked over the engine noise.

The soldiers ignored her.

"You must be proud," she said sarcastically. "Capturing two kids all by yourselves."

"Jamie?" I whispered. "What are you doing?"

"And it only took five of you," she said.

They still ignored her.

"Ixnay on the pissing them offnay!" I whispered. "They have guns."

"Hey, Bug," she said loudly. "Doesn't that one look like Elmer Fudd?"

Well, I didn't know her plan, but Jamie's always two steps ahead of me. So I said, "More like the Tasmanian Devil."

The guy smacked my head. "Shut up."

"Or Dilbert," Jamie said.

The guy smacked my head again. "Shut up."

"Hey!" I said. "That wasn't even me."

Which led him to smack my head.

Jamie opened her mouth to say something and—fortunately for my head—the truck rolled to a stop.

"We here already?" Dilbert asked.

"Yeah," a grizzled soldier said. "We're five minutes into a twenty-minute trip, and we're already there."

"Oh," Dilbert said.

"Keep an eye on the diaper brigade," the grizzled guy told him. Then he turned toward the front and called, "Any trouble?"

The driver's voice came back: "Just a routine stop."

"The diaper brigade?" Jamie said. "Is that the best you can do?"

The soldiers ignored her, and we sat silently, rumbling down streets, turning and turning until I'd lost all sense of direction . . . and the truck stopped again.

"End of the line," Dilbert said, drawing a finger across his throat.

Just trying to scare us, he didn't know how right he was: with Roach hacked into the government systems, I expected the soldiers were delivering us right into Hund's hands.

They dragged us off the back of the truck. I blinked in the sudden sunlight. I expected to be in a military compound or VIRUS's command center.

Instead, we were looking at something very familiar.

Jamie's house. We'd driven in a complete circle.

"What the—" the grizzled soldier said.

Then a metal-encased hand grabbed him by the scruff of his neck and tossed him into the truck. Hard. We heard a thump, then nothing.

Well, except two more thumps.

With all the soldiers in a pile, Larkspur turned to us. "You all right?"

Jamie showed him the handcuffs. "Except for these."

He snapped them like paper chains.

"Hey, Jamie," I said. "What was the plan, calling that guy Elmer Fudd?"

"No plan," she said. "I was just mad."

"Next time you want to express your feelings," I said, "make sure it's *you* getting smacked."

PLAN B? WHAT PLAN B?

"How long before they notice those soldiers are missing?" I asked.

"Fourteen minutes," Larkspur said. He's very precise.

He grabbed the uplink and we broke into the Coopers' house down the street—because Jamie's wasn't safe anymore—and gathered in Mrs. Cooper's home office. She's the webmaster for a local company, and a real techie.

At least, she *was*, before Roach scanned her in.

Jamie turned on her laptop. "Did the information transfer go okay?" she asked Larkspur. "You got the data?"

"What data?" I asked.

"*The* data."

"Wait," I said, staring at her. "You found Roach's real-world address?"

"She sure did," Larkspur said. "Dr. Solomon is scanning the files right now."

Jamie flashed me a superior look. "Not bad for a dragonfly that can't even shoot."

I was gonna say something witty, but right then, images started blurring across the laptop screen and my aunt's computerized voice said, "I've decoded the address."

She's not much for starting a conversation with *hello* these days.

Hello. I see no use in beginning a statement with a greeting instead of the pertinent information. Good-bye.

Very funny.

Anyway, she said, "I know the location of Roach's server. But there are two problems."

"Before we get the bad news," Jamie said, "where are Poppy and Cosmo?"

"That's the first problem. They jacked out twenty minutes ago, and I've been keeping them in a buffer ever since, repairing the damage."

"The damage?"

"See for yourselves."

And with that, Poppy and Cosmo shimmered into existence through the uplink. For a second, I thought they looked okay: a little battered and bruised, but okay. Then I saw the bluish electric field—about the size of a dinner plate—shimmering in the middle of Cosmo's stomach, and another one on Poppy's back, between her shoulder blades.

"I've repaired them as well as possible," my aunt said as the images on-screen dissolved and re-formed. "Yet complete recovery will take hours or days."

"Great," I said. "What's the other problem?"

"As you know, we located Roach's server site—"

Poppy perked up. "Then what're we waiting for?" She spun a throwing star on her fuzzy forefinger. "I've got something here for Hund."

"And we identified his time frame. Tonight he's going to transfer everything from his server to his virtual domain, where his cyber security is impenetrable."

"What does that mean for us?" I asked.

"If we don't download the data *today*," Jamie said, "and destroy his server, we'll never get this chance again."

"As a wise skunk once asked," Poppy said, "what're we waiting for?"

"You and Cosmo are not at full power," Auntie M said. "And Larkspur and I discovered that Roach is developing a new technology to deploy biodigital weaponry."

"Codenamed 'Cypher,'" Larkspur said.

"We suspect Roach used the new tech to give Commander Hund some impressive biodigital upgrades. He's a one-man army now."

"RoboHund," Cosmo said. "The Hundinator."

"Without time to train," my aunt said, "I don't know if we can win this fight."

Larkspur nodded slowly. "We don't have any other options, do we?"

"You can run," my aunt said. "You can hide. You can let the police and army fight Roach by themselves—and lose."

For a moment, nobody said anything. We just looked at each other in Mrs. Cooper's home office, in an empty house where the owners would never return.

"In that case," I said, "we've got no choice at all. We'll fight."

TRUCKIN'

I was back in the military truck, this time in the front seat between Cosmo and Jamie. Cosmo drove, trying not to jam my knees every time he shifted gears.

Ten blocks from the Coopers' house, Poppy asked, "How are we doing for time?"

Jamie yipped and I yelped. "Would you not *do* that?" I said.

Poppy cocked one fuzzy ear. "Do what?"

"Appear as if by magic," Jamie said, "hanging upside down from the roof, outside the passenger window."

We'd been driving toward the highway, silent. Of course, I'd had a hundred questions—Where was Roach's base? Did we have any chance of saving Jamie's parents? Would Auntie M find another way to reanimate herself? How many more biodriods did Roach control? What were Hund's upgrades? Where was I gonna live? What if we didn't destroy this server today? Were we going to *survive* until tomorrow? Talking skunks? *Really?* Could we call someone in the government to help? Did we have any chance of beating Roach? How powerful was VIRUS?—and I'm sure Jamie had even more. But this was a big moment. We were leaving town.

Leaving forever. No one had said that was what we were doing, but they didn't have to. There was nothing to come back to.

We'd lived there all our lives, more or less. The day before, we couldn't wait to leave; it was such a small town, and so lame.

But that day? I felt a lump in my throat, and I'm pretty sure Jamie was blinking back tears. Because that lame small town was our home. And we'd never go home again.

So imagine that thoughtful silence broken by Poppy—who hadn't been there a moment before—sticking her head in the window and asking, "How are we doing for time?"

"On schedule, as long as we don't hit traffic," Cosmo said. "Now get outta sight."

She vanished. Just like we were going to do. Well, after destroying the server. And rescuing Jamie's parents and all the other victims.

THE RATIO OF A CIRCLE'S CIRCUMFERENCE TO ITS DIAMETER

Jamie twisted in her seat and called out, "Is it safe to log on?"

From the back of the truck, where he was riding with Poppy, Larkspur answered, "Your satellite connection is secure."

"Thanks." She tapped a few keys.

"You're all intact?" my aunt asked through the laptop speakers. "Jamie? Doug?"

"Intact?" I said. "Yeah, we're okay."

"Hold one moment while I fix on your position. Cosmo?"

"Here," he said from the driver's seat.

"This is your optimal approach to Roach's server." She rattled off some coordinates. "Any questions?"

"Nope," Cosmo said. "Won't be long now."

"I have a question," Jamie said. "Why didn't the skunks travel digitally? They'd already be there."

"Two reasons," my aunt said, the screen a kaleidoscope of images. "First, my scans show that Roach created an ambush with dozens of new cyberdroids, which the skunks, in their current condition, would not survive."

"Oh. And number two?"

"We needed to remove you and Doug from town."

"Speaking of which," Jamie said, "what should we do at Roach's base while the skunks are downloading the data and destroying that server?"

"Keep yourself safe," Auntie M said. "And far from the fighting."

"But we can help! With the dragonfly and . . ." Jamie glanced at me. "Well, the dragonfly."

Great. She couldn't come up with any way I could help. I guess that made me the comic relief.

"Perhaps," Auntie M said.

"They're my *parents*," Jamie said tightly. "I want to help. I need to help."

"I will run simulations. Now I must withdraw, to finish the documents and prepare the transfer."

"What documents?" I asked after my aunt logged off. "What transfer?"

"The transfer is how we'll save everyone," Jamie said. "Before the skunks destroy the server, they need to capture all that data, all the scanned minds."

"Right, so we can reanimate everyone."

She shrugged, like she didn't care, but her voice caught a little. "Eventually. Once we get the technology."

"And the documents?"

"No idea."

I nodded slowly. "So the skunks break into Roach's base, download that data, and destroy the server. Right?"

"Easy as three point one four one five nine!" Cosmo said cheerily.

"Huh?" I said.

"Easy as pi," Jamie told me.

"Oh," I said, like I knew what she meant.

IN WHICH NOTHING EXPLODES, FOR ONCE

We drove for hours alongside the biggest cornfield of all time. Corn everywhere, and no buildings except a few grain silos. Then Cosmo pulled off the road and ran over rows of cornstalks, crushing them under the wheels. Probably leaving an emoticon crop circle.

"You sure this is the right place?" I asked, hopping from the truck when he finally stopped.

"Yeah," Jamie said. "This doesn't look like a high-tech evil genius headquarters."

Cosmo grinned. "That's what makes it such a *good* high-tech evil genius headquarters."

Larkspur came around the side of the truck. "The entrance is a mile to the north." He pointed through the corn. "We're just beyond Roach's outer perimeter."

"What's his inner perimeter?" Cosmo asked. "Cucumbers?"

Larkspur ignored him. "We have to move fast, but we can get there in time."

"Let's do this," Poppy said.

"'Let's do this'?" Cosmo echoed as they started off. "Isn't that a little generic?"

"Wait!" Jamie said. "What about us?"

"Dr. Solomon will fill you in," Larkspur said, and the three of them disappeared from sight.

Jamie and I stood there for a moment, watching the corn sway. Finally, we turned back to the truck, and Jamie grabbed her laptop and started to log on. Then she stopped and looked at me.

"Are you scared?" she asked.

"Scared?" I said. "Me? Why would I be scared? Because my aunt's gone and I almost got gutted by Hund, blown up by a nuke, scanned into a nightmare, arrested, beaten, and killed?"

"I'm scared, too," she said.

Far over the fields, the orange sun touched the horizon, and the quiet evening darkened. The sky looked huge, and a warm wind tiptoed through the cornstalks. It was beautiful.

For a moment, it felt like everything would be okay.

But we knew the truth. We knew what was really going on.

In the hidden sectors of cyberspace and on secret training bases, VIRUS was gaining power. With Roach's biodigital technology and Hund's mercenary army, they sought nothing less than scanning in the world—digitizing minds and ruling them as programmer gods.

Roach developed new technologies every day—technologies to overthrow governments and destroy countries—and there was no one to stop him.

Except us. Two kids, three skunks, and my digital aunt.

Jamie bit her lip. "What if we can't do this? Beat Roach, I mean. What if we can't win?"

"I can't even turn in my homework on time." I leaned against the truck. "But you *always* win."

"Me?"

"What'd you ever fail at?"

"Making friends." She looked toward the sunset. "Before you."

"That is so not true."

She shook her head. "You're always saying how ordinary you are. Why, because everyone likes you and you always fit in?"

"No, because—"

"If you hadn't been my friend, I *never* would've fit in. You were my . . . my passport. Once you liked me, suddenly I wasn't just some strange little geek girl anymore. So . . . thanks." She shrugged. "I wanted to say that."

I mumbled something. I'm not really good with that sort of thing.

"C'mon," she said, briskly logging on. "Let's see what your aunt says."

"No," I said. "Listen . . ."

"You don't have to say anything, Doug."

"I know, but . . ." This time it was me who shrugged. "If I had to get stuck in this whole mess with anyone, I'm glad it was you."

She started to answer. Then her laptop flashed a thousand pictures a second and she said, "Dr. Solomon?"

"Yes, Jamie?"

"How are the skunks?"

"Approaching Roach's headquarters," my aunt said. "Disabling the external security devices. They've overlooked a sensor."

NEXT TIME MAYBE TRY "AVOID IT"

Remember those grain silos I mentioned earlier?

They weren't silos.

They were outposts of VIRUS's underground command center, disguised as corn silos and grain bins. They contained satellite communication devices, ventilation shafts, and, of course, security systems.

Security systems that could detect a field mouse at two hundred feet.

Good thing the skunks weren't field mice. Cosmo knew security systems better than the people who'd designed them, and circumvented three layers of security without any trouble—except for one sensor.

"Wait," Larkspur said, raising his hand.

Cosmo looked up from the motion detector he'd been dismantling. "Hm?"

"Message from Dr. Solomon. You missed the lepton sensor."

"Patience, brasshopper," Cosmo muttered. "I'll get to the lepton sensor soon enough."

Thirty seconds later, he'd defeated that one, too, and they slipped into a silo.

"That's a lot of corn," Poppy said, looking around.

Larkspur peeled back a sheet of corrugated metal, stepped inside the gap and tore a hole in the floor, then dug through seven feet of packed dirt, until he hit concrete. He sounded like a couple of jackhammers. Good thing Roach put all his trust in the sensors and hadn't bothered with patrols.

Larkspur scooped away the concrete like it was wet sand,

tossing the chunks over his shoulder for Poppy and Cosmo to catch. After he'd dug a Larkspur-sized hole in the concrete, he turned to Poppy.

She grinned and dove—headfirst—inside, quiet and quick as a shadow sliding down a wall. She's part Ninja. Nobody moves more quietly or hides better.

Cosmo and Larkspur followed and found themselves fifty feet underground, in the shadows of an access tunnel.

"I hate this," Poppy said. "Skulking around like we're afraid of Roach and his little soldiers."

Well, she's part Hog Stomper, too. They favor the direct approach.

"We're not skulking," Cosmo told her. "We're *skunking*."

"You heard Dr. Solomon," Larkspur reminded her. "We're not at full power, and we're attacking Roach in his strongest spot. Stealth is required."

"Just point me toward the server and let me bust some heads."

Cosmo pointed to a yellow cable running nearby. "Is that a q-res data line?"

"Looks like," Larkspur said.

"Then let's follow the yellow brick road."

Larkspur nodded. "Should lead directly to the server."

They followed the cable through an underground maze of access tunnels until they found the main trunk line.

"Not far now," Cosmo said.

"This feels too easy." Larkspur checked his wrist monitor. "Where are Roach's defenses?"

The moment he said the last word, three figures emerged from the gloom ahead. Not security droids with robot arms but Roach's pet biodroids, like that monkeybeast in the Center. Except these were *Biodroids: The Next Generation*.

Imagine a combat android, not *that* different from Larkspur. Now imagine an orc. A stinking, flesh-eating orc. Now imagine that the android and the orc have kids. A drooling, armored, rabid, gene-spliced cybernetic nightmare.

Cosmo shot from the hip and a sticky black liquid hosed down the nearest droid, which gave an earsplitting shriek of rage and fear and ran away.

"What is that stuff?" Poppy asked as she spun in the air and kneed the second droid in the face.

"Uncle Cosmo's special sauce," Cosmo said.

Poppy slammed the droid three times, lightning fast, with her crowbar. It went down hard and didn't get back up.

Larkspur ducked a punch by the third droid and landed one of his own. The droid flew backward like it had been hit by a train. It smashed against the wall and fell to the ground.

"Have a Coke and a smile," Larkspur said.

Cosmo rolled his eyes. "That's only funny if you're throwing a soda machine."

"Oh," Larkspur said. But you could tell he didn't really get it.

Poppy looked down at the unconscious droids. "That was too easy."

"You always think it's too easy." Cosmo holstered his gun. "Even if you *lose*, you think it was too easy."

"No," Larkspur said. "She's right. Those droids weren't operating anywhere near full capacity."

"No?"

Larkspur consulted his monitor again. "More like ten percent of capacity. Roach is trying to draw us closer. Into a trap."

"So what do we do?"

"Spring it."

MR. NOBODY

Back at the truck, Jamie asked, "So what do *we* do?"

"I've altered your school records," my aunt said, "and generated several counterfeit airline tickets in your name."

"Um," Jamie said. "Why?"

"To establish that you've been visiting your uncle Charles and aunt Simone for the past four days."

"But those VIRUS soldiers saw me."

"No. They saw your twin sister."

"Is your circuitry all right?" Jamie asked. "I don't have a sister."

"The records now show that you do."

"Oh!" I said. "Those are the documents you were fixing?"

"Indeed. And they reveal that Jamie's *sister* was scanned into Roach's domain with her parents. You are clear, Jamie. You are not being sought by any agency. I arranged for a plane ticket to your aunt and uncle's house. You will stay with them."

"What are you talking about?"

"Live with your family. Enroll in a new school." I don't know if I imagined it, but the next thing my aunt said sounded just like the old Auntie M. "You can get your life back, Jamie."

"But . . . we're gonna rescue my parents, right?"

"My calculations indicate a 3.08 percent chance of success."

"Three percent?"

"And even if the skunks download the data, we cannot reconstitute the minds in the foreseeable future. The research will take months, or perhaps years, before—"

"Fine! I get it!" Jamie bit her lower lip. "What about VIRUS? What about Roach? What about the dragonfly? You need it for research."

"You can control the dragonfly from a remote location."

"Roach took my parents and destroyed my town. He's got plans for the rest of the country and I—I'm not running away."

Auntie M ignored her. "Unfortunately, Douglas, I cannot do the same for you. Instead, I deleted all digital evidence of you and assembled a new identity. You will live with the skunks, if they survive tonight's conflict. You will aid them with human interaction, and they will attempt to protect you."

That's the thing about my aunt now—sometimes she sounds cold. She talked about the skunks' survival like it was no big deal. She estimated a 3 percent chance of success and didn't break the news gently. And she ignored Jamie when she said she didn't want to live with her aunt and uncle.

At first, you might think she's sort of mean. She's not. She has feelings just like you and me. But she's also part computer. She can't always express her emotions that well.

Thank you for your understanding, Douglas. I do attempt to communicate in an emotionally appropriate fashion.

You're welcome.

Anyway, that was that. Jamie would live with her aunt and uncle, and I'd live under a new identity with the skunks. We'd probably be hundreds of miles apart. Maybe thousands.

"I'm not running away," Jamie said again.

"My calculations indicate that—"

Jamie cut her connection to Auntie M.

"Well, that was rude," I said.

"I'll apologize later." She booted up the dragonfly. "Maybe."

"What're you doing?" I asked.

"Showing your aunt how useful I am. If Roach has any surprises planned, I'll warn the skunks."

She guided the dragonfly into Roach's domain—easy now that she knew the way. She started rooting deep into the underlying digital structure, looking for anything that might help the skunks.

"Where are they?" I asked. "Can you bring them up on-screen?"

"Sure." She jiggled the dragonfly and tapped a few keys.

And we saw the skunks on the laptop's monitor.

"Oh, no," Jamie said. "They can't be . . ."

We looked closer.

"Are they . . . dead?" she whispered.

ON THE GRID

The skunks knew they were walking into a trap, but they didn't have any choice. In minutes, Roach would download the information on his server to his virtual domain. He'd never be this vulnerable again—and they'd lose their best chance to save all the scanned people.

So they traced the cables to the center of Roach's headquarters.

"Skunk 'em!" Cosmo yelled as they burst into the upper level of a underground bunker.

"Skunk 'em?" Poppy said, kicking the guards into the far wall.

"Yeah," Cosmo said. "That's our battle cry."

"How about 'rarin' to rummmmble!'?"

"Pardon me for interrupting," Larkspur said. "But we have a server to download and destroy."

He smashed through a set of double doors and led the other skunks into a room the size of an airplane hangar— where they stopped short.

The good news: they found the server.

The bad news: they also found a dozen biodroids, two dozen soldiers, and three dozen security drones.

Oh, and Commander Hund.

Upgraded. Enhanced. Augmented.

And pointing a weapon the size of a La-Z-Boy, with three barrels and laser targeting and— Well, actually, the thing reminded me of a carapace rifle in *Arsenal Five*.

"You're too late," Hund said. "We transferred the data an hour ago."

Cosmo dove sideways and drew his gun, but Hund was faster.

He pulled the trigger and hit Cosmo dead center. The impact smashed Cosmo into the blast wall that had slammed shut behind the skunks, and he slid to the floor unconscious, his fur smoldering.

Hund sneered and dropped his carapace rifle. "I won't be needing *this*."

Poppy sprang toward him. In one-to-one unarmed combat—and at full power—almost nothing can stand against her. Not even Hund. At least, not *before* his biodigital upgrades.

But now? Roach had turned him into a superpowered killing machine.

Poppy arced through the air and kicked Hund in the neck, hard enough to dent steel—but Hund just grabbed her ankle and threw her directly upward. She smashed into the ceiling at approximately 120 miles per hour.

Then she fell to the floor and stayed down.

"If I were at full power . . . ," Larkspur growled. He swung, but Hund caught his fist and started pushing Larkspur backward.

"I'd still win," Hund said.

He shoved Larkspur against the wall and pulled his knife. Not the same knife, though—even *that* had been upgraded.

He sliced through one of the cables in Larkspur's armor, and Larkspur crumpled.

Then Hund looked at the three motionless skunks.

"Dr. Roach," he said, nudging Cosmo's body with his foot, "your upgrades are more than adequate."

Roach entered from a concealed observation deck in the corner. "Precisely as I told you."

"With my upgrades, and the weapons from the Center, we could beat an *army*."

"Armies are the past, Commander. I care about the future." Roach rubbed his hands together. "Our workforce is busy expanding my virtual domain. Soon we'll be digitizing new subjects every day, reformatting and replicating them. The next step in human evolution. Streams of data flowing through electronic pathways, without the animal urges, the stinking fleshy—"

After a minute of that, Hund interrupted: "What should I do with the skunk-things?"

The manic gleam in Roach's eyes brightened. "They're a fascinating anomaly, the most advanced biodigital life-forms I've ever seen." He tapped at a command console, and a web of glowing lines appeared on the floor. "Toss them onto the grid."

Hund dragged the semiconscious skunks across the room.

"Skunk 'em," Cosmo muttered. "Dunk 'em."

"Junk 'em," Poppy moaned back.

Hund tossed them onto the grid and they fell silent.

Yet not completely motionless. The automatic-repair mechanism on Larkspur's suit sprang to life, welding his broken cable, working slowly and steadily, a tiny repair-bot shuttling inaudibly away.

Completely unnoticed.

Roach tapped at his keypad, and a nightmare dentist's drill slid from a metal housing near the grid and pointed at the skunks.

"Are you digitizing them?" Hund asked.

"Dissecting them," Roach said. "Taking them apart one line of code at a time."

"Will that destroy them?"

"Perhaps. If they survive, I'll reformat them—into loyal drones."

He flicked a switch and rays of blue light shot from the machine and pulsed around the skunks, growing brighter as the machine started to thrum loudly.

OFF THE CLIFF

"Are they . . . dead?" Jamie whispered.

Like I had any idea. "Check out Hund," I said.

He seemed kinda the same—huge and scary—and yet completely different. His implanted lens covered more of his face, and cables flexed beneath his skin. Looked like he'd gotten those biodigital upgrades he'd wanted.

I guess if Roach could create biodroids by splicing together genetically altered animals and military hardware, he could really do a job on a guy who was already a totally deadly mercenary fighter.

"Hund, version 2.0," I said. "That's all we need."

"Shut up! Look at the skunks, they're not moving. Look at them!"

I didn't want to look. I didn't want to admit how bad things were.

But I did. I looked.

And things were very, *very* bad.

All three skunks, battered and bleeding, lay slumped at Hund's feet while Roach tapped commands into a keypad nearby. A machine with a huge swiveling arm—that nightmare dentist's drill, tipped with laser scalpels and titanium pincers—hovered over the skunks.

They'd lost. They'd just . . . lost.

Which meant we *all* lost. Because without the skunks, *nobody* could fight VIRUS.

Nobody could stop them. Even after what they did to my aunt, and Jamie's parents—and all my neighbors, all my friends.

Nobody could stop them.

I stared at the screen, seeing the skunks helpless under Roach's machine and Hund upgraded into an invincible monster. And sure I'm a kid, but I'm not dumb: I knew that sometimes the bad guys won—maybe more than sometimes.

I watched the news. I knew that.

But I'd been scared to death for two days: I'd been bombed and handcuffed and chased by killers. I'd been shot and tear-gassed and I'd lost my home and family.

And I'd been terrified the whole time. I'd felt sharp jolts of adrenaline, but also a soul-deadening fear, the kind that makes thinking impossible. Because you don't want to think; you just want to curl into a ball.

Well, watching that screen, I reached the end of my fear, and like Wile E. Coyote hitting the edge of a cliff, I just kept on running.

I left Jamie outside—she must've thought I wanted to be alone to cry—and climbed into the truck. I adjusted the driver's seat. I didn't know much about driving, but I'd logged hundreds of hours on *Xtreme Racer 500*.

And I didn't care anymore.

So I turned the key and stomped on the accelerator. The engine roared, but I didn't move an inch.

I heard Jamie yell, "Bug!"

I stomped harder. Still nothing. Then I remembered the emergency brake.

I popped the brake and the truck shot forward.

They were a mile away. At this speed, that wouldn't take a minute.

The cornstalks blocked my view through the windshield.

I pressed harder on the accelerator, speeding blindly forward. The corn whirred past and flattened under the truck, and everything seemed okay.

Until a wall of corrugated steel loomed in front of me. A huge round grain bin.

I stomped on the brakes, but couldn't stop. I screamed and—

C R A SHED

into the wall.

And kept going. I smashed through and the seat belt slammed into me, and the front of the truck fell about ten feet, pointing almost straight down, into some kind of huge pit.

Well. *That* never happened on *Xtreme Racer 500*.

Then, with a *screeee*, the truck tore loose and started falling, still pointing straight down. I hadn't driven into a pit; I'd driven into a huge vertical shaft—and the truck dove toward the bottom.

Lucky for me, the shaft didn't end abruptly. Instead—

And lucky for you, you were wearing a seat belt.

That message brought to you by the Auntie M Safety Council.

Anyway, the shaft narrowed and slowly squeezed the truck to a halt.

When I finally remembered how to breathe, and trusted my legs to stop trembling, I climbed from the back of the truck, not quite sure what to expect, given how incredibly loud my stealth rescue mission turned out.

Fortunately, the worst of the noise coincided with the loud thrum of the dissection machine. And even more fortunately, when I climbed down a nearby maintenance ladder and opened the first door, I saw the skunks.

But not fortunately at all, they were still lying motionless on the grid. And Roach and Hund and a bunch of VIRUS soldiers were standing around, watching.

I guess I was feeling kinda crazy.

I shoved a wheeled tool cart toward the middle of the room, then ran the other direction, toward Roach. I didn't have a plan to stop him; I just figured I'd try to mess up whatever he was doing.

I ran fast and low, hoping all the soldiers would watch the tool cart roll across the floor. And it might've worked, except for one tiny detail: Commander Hund.

He was standing right next to Roach. Looming there, massive and deadly, his implanted lens scanning his surroundings.

And sure enough, in a flash, he'd grabbed me.

"You're a glutton for punishment," he said, and smiled his freaky smile.

"Not now, Hund!" Roach said. "I need you to keep the skunks on the grid."

Hund tossed me to one of his soldiers and looked at the skunks. Poppy and Cosmo were semiconscious and crawling toward the edge of the grid. So Hund kicked them back to the middle and sneered at Larkspur, who was curled tight in the center of the grid.

Larkspur looked like he'd given up, but really he was just waiting for his suit to finish repairing itself.

Still, what was he gonna do then? Hund had already beaten him. How could Larkspur save the day with Hund standing there?

That didn't occur to me until later, though. *Nothing* occurred to me right then—no thoughts, no plans, just a white-hot anger.

I started screaming at them. Swearing and shouting.

Fascinated by the dissection of the skunks, Roach bent over his monitor, his eyes bright, his fingers tapping, his tongue flicking between his lips. So I screamed even louder, just to distract him.

Not too bright, but I couldn't think of anything else to do.

He finally turned to the soldier holding me and said, "Shut him up."

The soldier put a gun to my head.

You know what?

That shut me up.

But I didn't get any less angry.

In fact, I got even angrier. I was helpless again, and I hated that. I hated Hund and Roach with a burning intensity. I stood there shaking with rage as the blue light zapped the skunks, dissecting them.

I found myself staring at Hund's huge gun, the one he'd dropped on the floor. I imagined I had a carapace rifle in my hand—

And something clicked.

In my head.

Across the room, a red light flashed on Hund's gun.

I focused on the light. I focused on the redness and my anger. The flashing got quicker and quicker. Then I heard a beep, a soft alarm.

Hund cocked his head. With his augmented hearing, he localized the sound in an instant. He grunted and stalked over to his gun. It must've weighed two hundred pounds, but he lifted it effortlessly, opened a console, and checked the readout.

The beeping came faster and louder. *Beep beep beep BEEP BEEP BEEP BEEPBEEPBEEPBEEEEEEEEEEEEEEEEEEEEEEEEEE EEEEEEEEEEEEEEEEEEEEEEEEEEEEEEEEEEEEEEEEEEEEEE* . . .

The soldier clenching my arm took a step backward. Then another. He knew something was wrong.

I heard a few soldiers mutter. Then one called, "Commander?"

The beeping changed to a buzz. Stopping and starting, like a short circuit. *Zzzt. Zt. Zzzzt. Zzzzzzzzzt. Zt.*

Then silence. Which sounded almost worse. Then sparks started shooting from the gun's console.

Someone yelled, "RUN!"

The soldier shoved me across the room and dashed for the exit.

In a sudden explosive lunge, Larkspur—his suit finally repaired—yanked the other skunks off the dissection grid, keeping his armored body between them and the sparking gun.

And me? I scrambled toward the door I'd entered through when the buzzing changed to a whine.

Hund hurled the gun across the room. "Evac! Evac!" he bellowed. "Roach—the evac pod!"

Roach slammed a button on his console and an evacuation pod burst from beneath the floor. Roach jumped into the pod, followed by Hund and a handful of soldiers, and the entry hatch slammed shut.

Meanwhile, I was racing toward the access tunnel. No idea why. I wasn't really thinking, just retracing my steps, I guess. I sprinted to the military truck—still wedged nose down in that huge shaft—and crawled in the back.

I flopped down, breathing hard . . . and realized how stupid I'd been. What was I gonna do, *fly* the truck outta there?

Which was when the gun exploded.

I'LL TAKE THAT AS A YES

Plumes of burning air poured up the ventilation shaft like lava erupting from a volcano, and pounded into the truck. Or maybe not like lava from a volcano, maybe like gunpowder in a barrel. Because instead of being incinerated, the truck shook and shuddered . . . then blasted from the ventilation shaft.

Straight into the air. Hundreds of feet into the air.

That was when I tumbled out the back.

So this is what happened: the gun went haywire, and I hid in the truck. Then a tremendous BOOM rocked the world, with flames and heat, and the truck jolted back and forth and finally turned upside down.

And I fell out the back and looked down and saw cornfields far below.

Only *then* did I realize I was in midair.

And

f
a
l
l
i
n
g

f
a
s
t

.

.

.

NEXT TIME, DIGITIZE FLYING SQUIRRELS

Larkspur yanked Cosmo and Poppy off the dissection grid, keeping his armored body between them and the beeping gun.

"Detonation in twenty-two seconds," he said.

"No . . . way out," Poppy said weakly.

"We know there's no way out," Cosmo muttered. "Thanks for the bulletin."

"I'll try to protect—" Larkspur said.

"No." Poppy pointed. "There. A way out."

Roach's evacuation pod rose toward the ceiling, and Larkspur understood immediately. He wrapped Poppy and Cosmo with one arm and leapt toward the pod.

Damaged and holding the two of them, he almost didn't reach the undercarriage in time. But he did, his fingers digging into the metal base. Barely. The pod emerged from the underground bunker and rose above the cornfields with the skunks clinging beneath.

Larkspur grunted. "Losing my grip."

"Um," Cosmo said. "Er . . ."

"What?" Poppy asked.

"There's a joke there somewhere," he said. "'Losing my grip.'"

The carapace rifle exploded far beneath them, sparking a chain reaction. Explosion triggered explosion, and the entire underground bunker detonated like the world's biggest Fourth of July show.

Larkspur lost his handhold.

They fell about five feet before the blast caught up with them and hurled them a hundred yards, where they dug three deep furrows through the cornfield.

For a moment, none of them moved.

Larkspur slowly stood. "Everybody functional?"

"I'm good," Poppy said, lying on her back, her fur still smoldering.

"Cosmo?" Larkspur asked.

"Skunk 'em," Cosmo muttered. He'd taken the brunt of the blast and was in tatters.

"Where's Bug?" Poppy asked. Then she answered her own question. "Sweet skunkin' samurai!"

She pointed high into the air, and Larkspur and Cosmo looked up and saw me.

Plummeting toward the ground.

Cosmo drew his gun and started spinning the cylinder. "I've got foam in here somewhere, could cushion the fall . . ."

"Not enough time," Poppy said. She looked at Larkspur. "Slingshot."

Larkspur grabbed her tail and spun around like a discus thrower—one, two, three, four times—then he hurled her toward me.

Meanwhile, I was dropping fast. I was too scared to be scared, if that makes any sense.

I was falling from the equivalent of a thirty-story building, but I wasn't screaming. What can you do? I was never gonna graduate. And forget about getting a driver's license.

Then I saw Poppy flying toward me. For a second, I thought she was really flying, like Superman—until she slammed into me, and I gasped and we fell together toward the earth.

"Not that I mind the company," I said, "but what do we do now?"

The ground was fast approaching. Poppy didn't have time to chat.

An instant before we hit, the fear finally kicked in. I screamed, and everything went black.

MAYBE A LOT MORE

Well, you know *I* lived, because I'm writing this. The good news is that Poppy lived, too. And so did Larkspur, Cosmo, and Jamie.

Is Auntie M alive? That's a good question. I'm not really sure. But my aunt is still with us, and she says we might be able to reanimate her if we ever beat Roach and VIRUS.

Right now, that feels like an awfully big *if*.

But I'm getting ahead of myself.

As you probably guessed, Poppy managed to cushion my fall. Nothing like video game reflexes and Hog Stomper toughness. Still, I got knocked around pretty good and blacked out.

I woke in the back of a cargo van, aching everywhere.

"Owwwwwwww," I moaned.

"Doug?" Jamie leaned over me. "How do you feel?"

I moaned again.

"Here." She held a bottle of water to my lips. "Drink."

I drank. "I hate water. You have any soda?"

"Have a Coke and a smile," Larkspur said, and laughed.

I gave him a dirty look, and everything went fuzzy.

The next time I woke, daylight shone through the windows in the back of the van. Jamie sat beside me, and Larkspur hunched nearby. Cosmo drove and Poppy sat shotgun. Fortunately, the van had mirrored windows.

After a rest stop and a handful of aspirin, Jamie filled me in.

"First," I asked, "where did this van come from?"

"Your aunt. Online rental is her *Arsenal Five*. She even arranged delivery a couple miles outside the cornfields."

"And where are we heading?"

She named a city I'd never visited.

"Oh."

"Yeah."

"Well, at least VIRUS headquarters was blown to bits."

She looked at me with bad news in her eyes.

"What?" I said.

"That was a temporary headquarters. Now that Roach transferred his data, he can set up anywhere in the country—"

"Or the world," Larkspur added.

I nodded slowly. "What about your mom and dad?"

Jamie took a deep breath. "Still trapped in his domain. All the people from town are."

I should've guessed, because her eyes were red from crying. "I'm sorry."

"There's more bad news," she said. "Roach still has the Protocol and his scanning booth technology."

"That was all for nothing?" I said bitterly. "Everything we did, everything that happened?"

"No," Cosmo said from the front, serious for once. "Roach threw his fastest pitch, and we knocked it outta the park. If you hadn't destroyed the HostLink, he'd have scanned half the country already. We stood up to him, we sprang his trap—and thanks to you, we walked away."

"And now we know what we're up against," Larkspur rumbled.

"That's right," Cosmo said. "All we need is some training, and we'll take VIRUS down. We have your aunt. We have Jamie and the dragonfly. We have you."

"Sure," I said. "Did you see how I kicked Hund's butt back there?"

"You saved our lives, Bug," Poppy said. "You drove that truck straight into Roach's base"—she looked proud—"and saved our lives."

"And if you ever do that again," Jamie said, tapping on her laptop, "and leave me behind, you won't have to worry about Hund, 'cause I'll kill you myself."

"I didn't do anything," I said.

"You were responsible for the gun malfunction, Douglas,"

my aunt said from the laptop. "Reconstructions reveal that you caused both the helicopter cable failure and weapon malfunction."

"How?" Jamie asked.

"The precise mechanism is unclear, though I presume that the Holographic Hub magnified Doug's inborn ability to cause . . . bugs."

"So he's a walking Bermuda Triangle."

"And he must learn to direct his ability to cause mishaps," Auntie M said.

"You're a one-man banana peel," Cosmo told me. "Mister Mishap."

Jamie laughed. "You always wanted to be a superhero."

"Captain Clumsy!" Poppy said.

So Cosmo's a commando fighter. Poppy's a martial artist. Larkspur's a tank. Jamie's a virtual reality hacker.

And me? I'm Stumbleboy.

Still, I looked out the window and I smiled. I guess I *had* saved their lives. And that's more than nothing.

THE NEW INDUSTRIAL PLANT

A week later we were still settling in.

We'd moved into an abandoned factory on the outskirts of a

new city. Auntie M bought it using false IDs and electronic money transfers and forged deeds. It was about the size of a football field, with three stories and an incredible assortment of old, rusty machinery. And it was in a broken-down industrial section, so no one had noticed when we'd made ourselves at home.

And no one noticed when my aunt started diverting shipments of high-tech hardware to our loading dock. For days, there was a constant stream of cutting-edge technology delivered to our front door.

Roach wasn't the only one who could put together a command center.

And you know what? I'm not gonna claim that we won: we didn't. But neither did VIRUS. Neither did Roach.

Instead of taking over the world in a week, he'd lost the HostLink. Instead of dissecting the skunks, he'd watched his temporary headquarters being destroyed. Instead of working in secret, he'll be exposed to the world. Because we're telling everyone about him. At least, we're trying to.

Sure, Roach had created cyberdroids and biodroids and a whole virtual domain. But he'd also created his own worst enemy: us.

He'd transformed me from an ordinary kid into . . . well, an ordinary kid whose best friend controlled a superpowerful hacking tool. An ordinary kid whose aunt became a digital Netform.

An ordinary kid who created the CyberSkunks.

We'd survived. We'd fought together and bled together and forged ourselves into a team. The skunks, me and Jamie, and Auntie M. And now we had a command center, with a training room and a firing range and more computer power than NASA.

Oh, and my aunt also arranged for furniture, clothes, food, and everything else. She was like a computerized compulsive shopper. She even bought a Harley for Poppy.

Auntie M enrolled me in a big city school, under a false name and address. I sometimes see that first-grade picture of me on the news; they tried to depict how I look now by "aging" the picture, giving me a pug nose and zits and mean eyes. But the drawing looks more like the Mole Man than me.

Jamie went to live with her uncle and aunt, who received a series of scary phone calls from government operatives ordering them not to ask questions about the explosion at the Center—or the disappearance of Jamie's parents and imaginary twin sister. The "government operatives" were really Auntie M, using voice-alteration software. She told Aunt Simone and Uncle Charlie to keep their heads down and live ordinary lives, for Jamie's protection.

At least Jamie lives only twenty minutes away, and we still go to the same school. It's not like being neighbors, but since she comes to the Ol' Factory most days after school, it's pretty close.

Yeah, I forgot to tell you about that: The Ol' Factory.

About ten seconds after we saw the place, Cosmo started calling our new home the Ol' Factory.

It's a pun. Say it fast. The Ol' Factory. The olfactory. Skunks living in the Ol' Factory.

Yeah, it's awful. But after a while the name sort of stuck.

Anyway, that's what happened. That's how I lost my school and my town and even my name and started living with skunk-people and a digital aunt.

And there's not much more to tell . . . right now. We're still hiding from VIRUS and hunting them at the same time. And not just VIRUS: there's more danger in the hidden sectors of the Net than anyone knows.

More on that later. Guess I'm done for now.

Oh, except one last thing.

I was daydreaming in class one day when something occurred to me. So when I got home, I cornered Cosmo.

"Remember when you were on that grid," I said, "with Roach dissecting you?"

"Sure."

"Well, you're skunks, right? So why didn't you . . . y'know?" I fanned my hand behind my butt.

"Do a chicken dance?"

"No, no. The thing is, skunks can, y'know, if they feel threatened or something, they can . . . stink."

He laughed. "You want to know why we didn't spray them?"

I nodded.

"You figure that regular skunks are stinky enough, right? So we should have chemical warfare stink bombs, huh?"

"Well, that's what I was wondering about." I was kind of embarrassed. It felt like a personal question. "So can you? Can you spray?"

"Sure. We *are* skunks, after all."

"Then why didn't you?"

"Because it stinks."

"That's the whole point."

"No, Bug. It's awful. Repulsive. Gross. Just because we're skunks doesn't mean we like the way it smells. You get that in your tail—phew!—you reek for a month. Dis*gusting*! You smell so bad you'd—"

Right then, the alarm sounded, and we rushed to the console.

"I'm tracking an unusually high level of secondary activity in one of Roach's encrypted sectors," my aunt said. "Looks like VIRUS is preparing something big."

The first thing we did was call Jamie and have her log on. Then the skunks jacked in while I—

Douglas. You assured me that you would complete your science homework before beginning another blog post.

I asked you not to scan my drive! Whatever happened to privacy?

I did not scan your drive. But your reaction confirms that you have not yet done your work.

Oh. Gave myself away, huh?

Let me just finish with this: Roach is still out there. Hund and VIRUS, too. Somewhere, lurking behind the codes and Web sites of cyberspace, they're out there.

Planning. Plotting. Preparing to digitize the world. To scan everyone in.

Even you.

But we're out here, too:

Me and Jamie, helping when we can.

My aunt, keeping watch.

And the CyberSkunks, battling in virtual reality and on the streets.

It's not an easy fight. Sometimes I think we can't win. But I promise you this: we'll never give up.

Oh, and one more thing: does anyone out there understand cell structure? I swear Mr. Lannister never covered any of this stuff in class.

All I need are the answers to questions one through seven on page 88 of *Elements of Scien—*

Good—bye. Be well. Eat your vegetables.

COMMONLY USED TERMS

ANFSCD: And Now for Something Completely Different.

BattleArmor: An ultrapowerful suit of combat armor made of an incredibly dense alloy for protection, with a built-in AI that provides enhanced speed and strength.

Digitized: Transformed from a living organism into computer code.

Holographic Hub: The main processing unit of the Center. The hub looks like an empty room but is actually seething with information. And it doesn't just crunch data; it optimizes all available code.

HostLink: A prototype device that can scan minds from a distance, thousands at a time. Designed as a research tool, but with the right modifications, the HostLink turns into a terrifying weapon.

Mainframe: A commercial-grade supercomputer capable of serving thousands of users simultaneously, often located in a secure, climate-controlled room.

Memory Cube: As big as a pack of cards, and with more memory capacity than ten thousand zip drives.

Modified stem-cell self-extraction media (aka "Steaks"): Although they look like T-bone steaks, they're actually the material from which digital files can grow into physical bodies.

Monkeybeast: An early version of Roach's biodroids. Imagine orangutans with elephant skin and glowing helmets for heads. And gun barrels sticking out of their armpits.

Motorcycle chain: Like a bicycle chain, but bigger and heavier. In Poppy's hands, a motorcycle chain is a deadly cross between a whip and a chain saw.

Protocol: Ultrapowerful software that transfers living minds into digital files.

Resloc: The virtual address of information in cyberspace. The location of some of Roach's most valuable data.

Scanning booths: Roach's triumphant technology, which digitizes not only minds but bodies. Looks like a glossy black Porta Potti with a shimmering door.

Steaks: See Modified stem-cell self-extraction media.

Uplink: A device that scans and transfers digitized information; hardware designed for use with the Protocol software.

Virtual reality: A computer-created "environment" that seems like a three-dimensional reality to users, who can see, smell, touch, taste, and feel inside the program. Like the holodeck on *Star Trek*, or the Danger Room in *X-Men*.

Virtual reality combat sim: A machine in which a soldier is immersed in various computer-generated combat scenarios for training purposes. Can be set to Nonlethal.

...the coffeemaker was so that...

...a big pot of sludge.

DOUGLAS SOLOMON

PLEASE RESPOND

?

I huddled over the coffeemaker and whispered, "Hello?"

In a moment, the display changed.

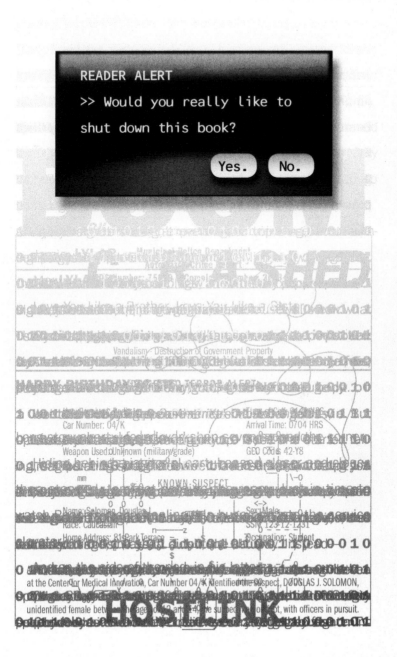

READER ALERT

>> Would you really like to shut down this book?

Yes. No.

ABOUT THE AUTHOR

The author of several books for adults, **joel naftali**, was surprised to receive an e-mail from someone claiming to be notorious fugitive Doug Solomon. Although he cannot vouch for the accuracy of this book, and does not endorse any illegal activity, Naftali agreed to help Doug find a publisher. Naftali lives in Maine with his wife and son and lawyer, who instructed him to mention he's cooperating fully with the authorities.